SUKI

SUKI

Suniti Namjoshi

PENGUIN
VIKING

ZUBAAN
128 B, 1st Floor, Shahpur Jat, New Delhi 110 049, India

in collaboration with

VIKING
Published by the Penguin Group
Penguin Books India Pvt. Ltd, 11 Community Centre, Panchsheel Park, New Delhi 110 017, India
Penguin Group (USA), 375 Hudson Street, New York, New York 10014, USA (a division of Penguin Group (USA) Inc.)
Penguin Group (Canada), 90 Eglinton Avenue East, Suite 700, Toronto, Ontario, M4P 2Y3, Canada (a division of Pearson Penguin Canada Inc.)
Penguin Group (UK), 80 Strand, London WC2R 0RL, England (a division of Penguin Books Ltd)
Penguin Group (Ireland), 25 St Stephen's Green, Dublin 2, Ireland (a division of Penguin Books Ltd)
Penguin Group (Australia), 707 Collins Street, Melbourne, Victoria 3008, Australia (a division of Pearson Australia Group Pty Ltd)
Penguin Group (NZ), 67 Apollo Drive, Rosedale, North Shore 0632, New Zealand (a division of Pearson New Zealand Ltd)
Penguin Books (South Africa) (Pty) Ltd, Block D, Rosebank Office Park, 181 Jan Smuts Avenue, Parktown North, Johannesburg 2193, South Africa

Penguin Books Ltd, Registered Offices: 80 Strand, London WC2R 0RL, England

First published by Penguin Books India and Zubaan Books 2013
Copyright © Suniti Namjoshi 2013
Illustrations in text and on cover © Joy Gosney. Leaf motif design © Anita Roy

All rights reserved
10 9 8 7 6 5 4 3 2 1

ISBN 978 93 83074 10 5

Typeset in Bembo 11/15.3 by Jojy Philip, New Delhi 110 015
Printed at Replika Press Pvt. Ltd, India

For Gill and Martin
who also loved Suki

DEAF EURYDICE
For Suki d. 27 July 1997

Sometimes the murmur of longing is so
tentative, and the thought of a caress so
tangential, that the senses strain to hear what,
after all, cannot be said.

And it's then that
the temptation arises: to write a lie
on the water, scribblings on sand, or to descry
from the way the leaves moved and the light
fell what shadows portend. This is twilight
time, Orpheus time, Demeter time, when they
call the long dead, and deaf Eurydice
struggles to hear and hearing nothing, falls behind
till her footfall makes no imprint save on the mind.

Contents

Part I: A Memoir

Part II: The Vipassana Trek

PART I
A Memoir

1

A Fearful Wight

I want to write down everything I can remember about Suki. Not to immortalize her (or myself). Books about cats are popular so she might gain a brief immortality, but 'brief immortality'? The vipassana teacher says one must have detachment. Vipassana is a form of Buddhist meditation — it means 'clear seeing'. According to the teacher one is unhappy because one does not have what one wants. And one is unhappy because one loses what one was happy with. He says all the Hindu sages say so. Also the Buddha. Well, yes, but…

I realized how much I mattered to Suki (and therefore she to me?) when we came back from America. The Buddhist teacher tells a story about a great king who was a great vipassana meditator. He asked his queen who she loved best in the world. She was supposed to say, "You, Sire," but she was also a great meditator, so she told the truth and said she loved herself. And the king – because he was a good chap and a great vipassana meditator – replied, "I was thinking much the same thing myself," and wasn't cross with her at all.

So given these caveats and provisos Suki and I loved each other. Suki was lodged in a cattery when we went to America for a few weeks to teach a course or two and earn some money. The people who ran the cattery were kind: they sent me a photograph of her, and they cuddled her every day. They had peacocks in the garden, and heaters in every cell. We called it Suki's Hotel. But when I returned from America and brought Suki home, she looked like a creature who had regained paradise long after all hope had been lost. I half explained to Suki that cats do not understand paradise, or she overheard me thinking it. The following day, when she was a little recovered, she snapped at me. "It doesn't much matter whether cats understand the Christian paradise or any other paradise. It doesn't even matter whether I agree with you that this is definitely a post-lapsarian universe and that you and I are living in a fallen world. Just don't do it again." Then she burrowed her face in my arm. "I missed you," she said. "And I you," I replied.

But the day after that when she was lying under the lilies, she murmured, "You only love me because you're not afraid of me."

"There may be some truth in that," I answered.

I had realized some time ago that I was 'a fearful wight' – a frightened creature, like Chaucer's Cressida. Frightening things, e.g. floods, fires, giant crevasses, force nine gales, earthquakes that measured 7.9 on the Richter scale, all these things frightened me – to a reasonable extent; but people terrified me. I don't know if Suki realized that. She was also 'a fearful wight'. The rages she flew into – especially at the vet's – and the murderous growls that issued from her throat were a sign of that. And she was a courageous wight too. Once she took on five cats while I was away. The cats had come with the new tenants next door. Fortunately, they moved away soon. My poor Suki. I found pieces of her fur on the grass.

True, we were both fearful; but when the fear didn't make us run away fast or paralyse us like rabbits caught in the headlights, it galvanize us into action. The idea was to look so confident and capable – capable of almost anything – that no one would dare mess with us. Once, after strapping her into a pretty red harness and attaching a lead, I took Suki for a walk. She terrorized all the dogs she could see. I'm not sure how she did it. She was only tiny. I think she strained at the lead and growled from deep within her throat, "Meat for the leopard! Meat for the panther! I eat stupid dogs!"

I don't know if Suki was afraid of people. Of course she was. Consider what used to happen regularly at the vet's. Or consider the small boy who had been given

Suki when she was still a kitten. He adored Suki and his elders adored him, and so he treated Suki as if she were his teddy bear or personal rag doll. In consequence he terrified Suki. When I came to live with them, I stopped all that. I pointed out that she was not, in fact, a toy animal, and they were entirely reasonable: they agreed that she was not. Well, perhaps not the boy – perhaps one needs to grow up before one can tell the difference between a plaything and a person.

Anyway, I was thinking all this and Suki was dozing or thinking whatever she was thinking, when she sat up and yawned and blinked at me in a solemn and friendly fashion. 'A little conversation,' I thought. 'She's ready for a few seconds of conversation.'

"You know," she said lazily, "I think you care about me because you are not threatened by me."

I squared up to that. "And you? Do you love me because you are not afraid of me?"

I thought I had phrased the question cleverly. She would probably have to say she was not afraid of me and that (therefore) she loved me. She could deny both, of course – fear as well as love – but the syntax made it harder. She beat me though. All she said was, "I am not afraid of you."

"You ought to be!" I retorted. "I'm about ten or twenty or thirty times bigger than you!"

"How do you figure that?" she asked, as though it was merely a matter of scientific interest.

"Weight," I replied.

"Let's face it, " I told her one day. "The reason we get on is because we're a pair of murderous animals and we acknowledge it." I had lapsed – once again – from being vegetarian and was trying to think profound and moral thoughts about the food chain.

Suki wasn't having any of it. "I don't spend my time committing murder," she told me. "I spend it sleeping."

"Well, that's a waste of time!"

"When I sleep, I dream."

"What do you dream about?"

"About life," she replied in a superior fashion. "Dreams are a reflection of life, like the landscapes reflected in a lake. In my dreams I am ten times bigger than you, but I don't bully you or pick you up by the scruff of the neck. Well, I only do it when you're being naughty, and anyway, I support you underneath. On the whole I'm nice to you and look after you and keep you out of mischief."

"Oh, don't be absurd, Suki," I replied. "How can I be 'naughty'? That's just a misunderstanding..."

"Precisely," she smiled.

I didn't want to quarrel with her. It was a day early in spring, the sun was shining and the grape hyacinths glowed like points of purple light. "Listen, Suki! I had a dream in which the two of us were equal."

"I'm as equal as you are – at least in my own mind," she said slyly.

"No, I mean really equal."

"What? The same size?"

I hadn't meant that, but I said, "Yes, the same size."

"Then what happened?"

"Well, there we were, me and my cat walking –"

"If we were equals, then I wasn't your cat," Suki interrupted.

"Well, all right. There we were, me and my sister, walking –"

"I'm not your sister!" Suki interrupted.

"I think of you as my sister," I said humbly.

"Well, all right," Suki relented.

"There we were walking down the road on our way to London to seek our fortune."

"If I had really been as big as you," Suki muttered, "the two of us would have taken up half the road. Or a circus trainer would have come along and tried to kidnap me."

"You're ridiculous. And you make up the most absurd things."

"I learnt it from you," she said. "You told me that that's what being a writer means."

"I said no such thing!"

"Anyway I don't want to seek my fortune. I like it down here."

"What will you do for money?" I asked nastily.

"Cats don't need money," she replied loftily.

I was feeling cross enough to want to make her face brutal reality. "The truth is," I told her, "cats don't have money. You're dependent on me to feed you."

"Yes," she replied equally nastily, "and what does that say about life and death and the nature of the universe?"

Then we didn't talk to each other for a whole hour, then we got bored and started talking again.

"I have friends among my own kind, you know," Suki informed me one day. "It's not as though I'm dependent on you."

"Oh yeah? Your own kind beat you up."

"I beat 'em back," Suki said proudly. "And anyway, you don't let me make friends with them. You're too possessive."

"Who came running into the house the other day and dived into my arms?"

"That was different. I was running away from two ferocious dogs, a wolf and a bear."

"A wolf and a bear? Are you sure half a dozen lions weren't also involved?"

"Yeah, half a dozen lions. You get the picture."

"And which of these creatures were you planning to make friends with?"

"Not those creatures, fellow cats," Suki said impatiently.

"Very well," I said somewhat huffily. "The next time you summon me into the garden to shoo away someone, I won't come."

"You haven't understood anything," Suki replied sorrowfully. "I was trying to explain that I'm not actually a misogynist or a misanthropist or a Disliker of Other Denizens of the Galaxy."

"Dogs!" I snapped. "You hate all dogs."

"I have done my very best to be fair to the species. Do you remember the time you sat in the living room with me on your lap and Chérie – Sherry? How can someone that big be called Chérie? – anyway, she sat on Juliet's lap and all of you tried to conduct a calm conversation so that Sherry and I would grow to tolerate one another in an atmosphere of peaceful amity?"

"Well?"

"Well, it worked, didn't it? You all looked so silly, it was impossible to snarl. Frail Juliet with large Sherry sprawled uncomfortably all over her lap, you looking determined and as though you were engaged on a noble mission, and Lucy and Gill doing their best to talk peacefully about nothing at all!"

"You're very intolerant," I told her.

"On the contrary," she said. "I put up with it all, didn't I? Dogs aren't supposed to sit on anybody's laps."

"Lap dogs?"

"Genetically engineered and hothouse trained."

"What are dogs supposed to do then?" I asked mildly.

"They're supposed to guard the perimeter of the Caretaker's estate," Suki replied without a second's thought.

"The Caretaker's estate?"

"Well, my estate then," she amended quickly. "The Caretaker – you – looks after the estate, and dogs are for guarding the perimeter."

I didn't know what to say, so I changed tack. "If

you are such a lover of all manner of galactic life," I demanded, "why did you bite that man's nose?"

"Which man?" she asked sweetly.

Now she had bitten several people's noses, so I just said, "The last one."

"You know why," Suki replied. "He kept trying to nuzzle me, even though you had warned him about it. He was trying to prove he was irresistible to cats."

"Suki, you made him bleed!"

"Only a little. Besides, I bite your nose too."

"You only nibble it and only when I'm standing on my head."

"Well, there you are then."

"Where am I?"

"Standing on your head, and afraid to topple over in case you crush me."

"And what does that prove?"

"I don't know," replied Suki. "I wasn't trying to prove anything."

2

Days

If I had asked her when I could have asked her, "Suki, if I do a biography of you, what would you like me to put in it?" she would probably have said, "Oh, I don't know, the usual thing; 'much loved and very loving'." She would have been sitting on my desk under the reading lamp. She liked to use it as a sun lamp. And perhaps she'd have put her head to one side and blinked.

I'd have persisted. "No, seriously, what sort of thing do you want me to put in it?"

"It depends on who you're writing it for," Suki would have replied. "You know – which market, audience, perfect reader – all that stuff you've told me about. It's no use asking me because you're not writing it for me."

Then she would have curled up on her orange shawl

in the top right-hand drawer of my desk and gone to sleep. She never was very interested in anything I wrote. Sometimes, she would listen politely while I tried out a poem, but that was only out of niceness.

Between the 2nd of June 1984 and the 27th of July 1997 it's exactly 13 x 365 + 55 + 3 (for leap year) days, that is 4,803 days. These are the days of Suki's life. Not a great many. There are probably more leaves on the giant ash tree growing against the bank in the adjoining field. And what's more, the tree sheds its leaves each year and grows them again. There's probably a moral or a miracle in that, but I don't know what it is.

Gill says to me I should be comforted because Suki had a happy life. I don't know what Suki would have said to that. On one of these 4,803 days – it was a day in January, we were still eating Christmas leftovers and I had lit a fire because Suki liked fires – anyway, on one of those January days, I said to her, "Suki, do you realize that your name means 'happy'?"

Suki purred.

"Suki, are you a happy cat?"

She purred some more.

"Suki, I don't want you to purr. I want you to attend to what I'm saying. Do you realize that 'Suki' is a Western mispronunciation of the Sanskrit 'Sukhi' which means 'happy, fortunate, contented'? What do you think of that?"

"I don't much mind," Suki answered. "Now do let

me enjoy the fire." And instead of purring, she began to snore. Perhaps she was only pretending to snore. It wasn't much use asking Suki if she was happy. She would just say how she felt at the moment. But then so would I, I suppose, if someone asked me how I was.

On a different day – this was in June. We had just got back from the vet. Suki had spent an hour sulking. Then I had spent the next two hours on my knees begging her to swallow her worming pill. I think she had made up a rule in her head that after I had said 'please' a thousand times she would swallow it. When she finally swallowed the pill, I patted her on the head

"There. That's a good cat,"

She didn't like that – too patronizing.

"I didn't do it out of virtue!" she retorted. "I did it because I was exasperated to death!"

That made me cross. It was all very well indulging Suki, but she had to understand what was what and who was boss.

"You have to do what I ask you to do, not expect me to be governed by your silly whims, you know," I told her sternly.

"Whims!"

"Yes, you have whims and I have well considered opinions and ideas."

"Rubbish!! Look, here's the bottom line. Who knows more about being a cat, me or you?"

And then she did what she always does when she thinks she has won an argument, she shut her eyes and went to sleep. Then she sat up again. "Anyway," she added, "you are governed by my whims."

"What do you mean?" I demanded.

"Well, this morning I made you open the front door five times so that I could run in again through the cat flap at the back. And if I hadn't got bored, you'd have probably done it six times or seven times or who knows how many times."

I was so outraged, I couldn't think of anything to say. Suki looked very pleased with herself.

On my fiftieth birthday Suki caught a mouse. It would have been Leaf No. 2,500 and something out of Suki's days. She would have been seven years old in a few weeks. It was a day in late spring. A few friends had come to celebrate. We were planting a magnolia tree in the front garden. Lucy was watering it with champagne. (I don't know why. She doesn't like wine very much; perhaps it was a libation.) Whatever she thought of dogs and other cats, Suki quite liked having human beings around. They usually made much of her and she was usually charming to them (aside from the matter of biting noses). Suddenly she trotted away and came back and deposited a mouse in the middle of the circle of my friends.

"Suki!" I glared at her. "You know perfectly well you're not supposed to catch mice!"

Suki looked obstinate. There she was a small lilac Burmese like a little statue personifying Obstinacy, just sitting there in the centre of that circle of friends.

"You know perfectly well why I caught that mouse. You're very unreasonable on the whole subject. I thought perhaps your friends would help you to understand. Do you really want to live with a whole load of mice?"

"That wasn't a house mouse, Suki. That was a field mouse. Just your presence, your very emanations, drives house mice away."

"Huh!" was all she'd say to that.

I picked her up and locked her up in the downstairs bathroom. Then Juliet and I took the half-dead mouse to the compost heap and I put an end to its life with the sharp edge of a shovel.

After a little while I let Suki out. She had explained to me once that there wasn't much point in locking her up for very long. She just went to sleep, she said. And if she was locked up for a very long time, she just got hungry, and even in prisons where people were serving long sentences for heinous crimes, starvation was never used as a punishment.

"Do you realize," Suki informed me one day, "that I am a goddess, this is a temple and you are my high priestess?" This was in her tenth year, when she was inclined to be a little blasé sometimes – Leaf No. 3,000 and something.)

"Do you realize," I replied, "that this is modern Britain, and not ancient Egypt or whatever time and place, probably imaginary, in which you think you were worshipped as a goddess?"

"Well, who am I then?"

"You're a bumptious little cat, who talks too much and spends all her time with me."

"Huh! The truth is you spend all your time with me. Anyway that makes me your familiar and you a witch!"

"I'm not a witch!"

"More's the pity."

"And who is Gill then?"

"Well, if I were a goddess, she could be your co-high priestess. It's grander than just a coven of witches."

"Can't you just be an ordinary cat in an ordinary household?"

"The Discreet Charm of the Bourgeoisie?" Suki asked sweetly. "Is that what you hanker after?"

"Listen," I said, "Hilary told me that her cat, Millie, comes in from the garden in a flurry of petals; and then wherever she walks, she leaves petals behind. Megastars and movie stars probably have rose petals strewn in their path as they stroll down the red carpet, but to leave petals in your footsteps – that's really something!"

Suki blinked, curled up and went to sleep. "You're easily impressed," she murmured sleepily.

It's not that there were no rules or that Suki won all the battles. There were laws, commandments even. I actually laid down the law when she returned to me again. I told her decisively and forcefully, though not right away, what the three things were that she absolutely must not do. She needed time to recover first. Because I hadn't wanted the boy to torment her with his rag doll treatment and because I wasn't sure that I could prevent it – I was going to be away for a year – I thought it best to let Suki go. But the household in which Suki stayed had another cat and the owners of the two cats eventually began to get on less well, and then that became true of the cats as well. And the result was that poor Suki suffered and became a neurotic and very badly behaved cat. She shitted where she ought not to, peed here and there – that sort of thing. Next she went to another household. These people had a number of other pets including a dog. After a while they explained to Gill and me that we would either have to have Suki back or they would have to look for another home for her or hand her over to the RSPCA. "You see," they explained, "Suki doesn't like to have any other cats or, indeed, any other pets around. She's the sort of cat who has to be the sole cat in the household."

I didn't respond to that. It wasn't very flattering to Suki, but then I didn't see why she had to be a sociable cat. What I did do was explain to the boy that we could have Suki back, but that he absolutely must not harass her in any way. He must not even stroke her or pat her or attempt to feed her without my express permission. As he was a little older now and understood why his attentions might be damaging to a small cat who was already a bit of a wreck, he agreed and he did stick to the agreement. The fact that he was away at boarding school helped. The people in the second household had done a great deal, despite the presence of the dog, to calm Suki down; and, after a few weeks of being back with Gill and me, she was all right again.

I explained to Suki once that she still had a few bad habits, e.g. the murderous growling at the vet's, and the little matter of not retracting her claws sufficiently when she jumped on my lap. She pointed out that she was a highly bred, highly pedigreed, lilac Burmese and that in consequence a little temperament was only to be expected. It reminded me of my grandmother telling a policeman in New York who scolded her for scattering peanut shells on the street that she was a gentleman lady and that he ought not to be talking to her like that. Pedigreed cats, revered grandmothers – perhaps it's all the same really.

Had Suki been sitting beside me just now, she might have said I was digressing. I think she thought I wasted a great deal of time yoking unlikely things together and speculating about what if and whether and what might have been.

And about her claws Suki maintained that she was doing me a favour by letting me clip them. I didn't concede that, of course, but it did worry me sometimes that I was depriving her of her weapons. What if she got into a fight in the garden?

One day she peed neatly exactly next to the toilet. She looked up at me and said, "Look, I've worked it out. This is how it's done, isn't it? In the bathroom." I scolded her, and punished her. Later I realized I had got it all wrong. I felt ashamed. I should have set up a litter tray there. I apologized of course, but she was annoyed. She went out. When she came back and I apologized again, she shrugged philosophically. "Apartheid," she said. "Sometimes it just erupts suddenly between species."

Once I said to Suki, "If there were a war between cats and human beings, whose side would you be on?"

"Whose side would you be on?" she shot back at me.

I didn't want to answer, but she read my thought anyway. That's how we communicated mostly, together with body language and the odd bit of sound. I was thinking that I would be on Suki's side, but I would have to pretend otherwise to the people around me.

"I don't have to pretend anything to anybody," Suki said smugly. "I would just be on your side because I felt like it. I'd perch on your shoulder like a proper Burmese cat and claw the enemy."

"What enemy?" I asked wonderingly.

"The other Burmese cat perched on the other warrior, silly. That's what Burmese cats used to do, you know."

I decided she was just making it up as she went along.

"That's what you do!" she shot back at me. "And anyway, I wasn't making it up. I'm sure you read it somewhere."

"I read it somewhere?"

"Yes," Suki replied. "You read books and tell me the interesting bits. It saves time."

I have no proper photographs of Suki, only a couple of snapshots. Perhaps I thought she would live forever. Would I have taken photographs if I had had a strong and recurrent sense of her mortality (and of my own)? What would I have said? "Suki, we are mortal. Therefore I am going to photograph you." She would have laughed.

Or perhaps she would have pointed out that I didn't have a camera. In those days I didn't. Or perhaps she would have said, "Wait. You had better brush me first. And I'll have the green collar instead of this yellow one. It suits me better." She wouldn't have said all that about collars. She wasn't vain or in the least self-conscious, just fastidious.

3

Rules and Commandments

Sometimes Suki, or the memory of Suki, sits so lightly on my shoulder that it's as though she's back.

"Go on," she prompts. "You have to say what the three commandments were. And then, if I feel like it, I'll tell you the rules I made up for you."

The commandments were simple enough. The first one was that she was not to go out of the garden, and especially not through the front gate.

"I wasn't stupid, you know. I wouldn't have been killed."

"No, Suki. You weren't stupid, but the drivers of motorcars are stupid. You might have been killed."

"Anything might have happened," Suki mutters.

She only broke that commandment occasionally.

"Huh! I only broke it when I was sure you could see me breaking it, so that you would stop working and come into the garden."

I had suspected that. The second commandment was that she was never to jump in through the kitchen window, because then she would land on the oven hob and it might be hot and she might get burnt.

"Truly idiotic," Suki puts in. "The kitchen window was always shut. How could I have possibly jumped in through it?"

I can't remember how or why that commandment got made. "I'd have thought you'd have been glad to have had a commandment you could obey so easily," I say crossly.

Suki, or rather the memory of Suki, thinks that's so outrageous, she falls off my shoulder. Then I remember.

"Suki, the real commandment was that you were never to jump on the oven hob."

"I never did," she replies haughtily.

And the third commandment was that she was never to catch birds or mice.

"You realize, of course," Suki remarks, "that in obeying that one, I indulged you. It was completely irrational."

"It was not!" I retort. "I couldn't very well put out peanuts for the birds, and then have you go out and nab the birds. It would have been – it would have been" – I search for a word – "perfidious."

"Oh my, 'Perfidious'," Suki mocks me.

"Yes," I reply, "like the big game hunters in India in the olden days when they tied a small goat under a tree and sat in the branches on a machaan and shot the tiger when it came along."

"You feel," asks Suki, "that they should have allowed the tiger to eat the kid?"

"No, of course not. It's just −"

"It's just that you're squeamish. I didn't catch birds, and you went out and bought chickens, which someone else had killed, and which had probably grown up in total misery on some battery farm, and then you roasted them and boned them and chopped them up into small pieces and fed them to me. You do see, don't you, that you're not making much sense?"

"I did it for your sake," I respond feebly.

"Rubbish!"

"Well, but Suki when the vets all recommended that especially prepared dry food, I stopped the chickens and gave you that instead."

"And you think that was an improvement? It tasted like cardboard and was probably the cause of my eventual diabetes!"

I'm beginning to feel so bad about the whole thing I don't say anything, but Suki hasn't finished yet.

"And do you remember the day − Leaf 5,074 in your reckoning −"

"Suki, you only lived for 4,803 days."

"There you are."

"Where am I?"

"There you are being absurd. Moses would have laughed himself silly."

"Moses?"

"Yes, the Ten Commandments wallah –"

"Suki, where did you pick up your vocabulary?"

"Mostly from you. As I was saying before you interrupted me, do you remember the day a swift or a martin or some such bird flew into the house? First you locked me up, then you let me out and then you said to me, 'Please Suki, find the bird, but don't catch it or kill it.'"

"Suki," I reply earnestly and admiringly, "you found the bird in two seconds flat perched on a lampshade; and then you pointed at it as perfectly as any pointer."

"I do not point like a pointer!" Suki snaps. "As a matter of fact cats don't point. And anyway I only did it to oblige you."

"And I was then and still am deeply grateful," I say politely.

But she still isn't done. "And then what about the time there was a mouse in the living room?"

"Er, well, yes, you were –"

I'm about to say 'heroic', but she interrupts me. "You know, you are very trying sometimes. First you locked me up – as usual. Then you let me out and asked me to sit still and head the mouse towards you, while you ran about trying to catch it. You were quite hopeless.

And then you gave up and said, 'Please Suki, I'm not fast enough. Would you mind cornering it and catching it, but not killing it?'"

"You did precisely that," I acknowledge humbly. "You were a remarkably adroit and astute cat and exceedingly good-natured and kindly."

"Yes, and I also did a pretty good job of training you, you know," Suki adds smugly. "And that wasn't at all easy."

"What do you mean?" I expostulate. "You trained me? It's supposed to be the other way about. And anyway, what do you mean I wasn't easy to train?"

"You're getting muddled," Suki says with some satisfaction because I've fallen into her trap. "If you're saying you didn't get trained, that just proves how impossible you were and how unwilling to understand and to compromise. And if you are saying that you were easy to train, then that establishes surely that you were trained, and indicates, furthermore, that I did an excellent job of making it easy for you."

I am so annoyed by this time, I decide to sulk; but Suki usually has a pretty good idea of what I'm thinking, so she says hastily, "You weren't nasty or ill-mannered or anything like that, but you were slow. For instance, it took me ages to get you to open the front door when I wanted you to open it. You seemed to think the cat flap would do. I couldn't understand why you couldn't understand that a cat flap and a front door are two different things."

"Did you know," I tell her, hoping to smooth things over, "that when Rita Gircour boasted that her cats were so intelligent they could open the fridge, Gill told her that you were far cleverer and got me to open it."

For some reason Suki is embarrassed by the compliment. "That was just good manners on your part," she says lightly.

Perhaps I can get in a small protest. "Suki," I say, "when you had your very own cat flap, was it reasonable of you to make me open the front door?"

"Perhaps not," she replies, "but it was fun." Then she adds, "Towards the end the cat flap was getting difficult for me."

That hurt. "Oh Suki!" I cry and reach up to lift her down gently onto my lap, but she has vanished. Shades, ghosts, memories are insubstantial after all.

After she died the clock clattered on. I still sit at the same desk, weed the same garden – no Suki though to sit among the tulips or doze under the lilies or just sprawl on the grass with me when the sun happens to shine.

I wonder what rules she made up for me. As I sit here thinking I realize that one of her rules was that I had to be present when she had her food. Sometimes I'd put out her breakfast late at night so that she wouldn't have to wait for me to wake up in the morning. But she did wait. I would wake up to find her sitting on my pillow looking down at me: her large golden eyes shining, her paws placed neatly in front of her, her lilac fur looking well brushed. She always waited for me to open my eyes before she said anything and was never cross or impatient. We would go downstairs slowly, and I would give her her food in a clean bowl and also some fresh water. I would then introduce her to her food and the food to her: "Food, Suki. Suki, food." She must have thought this was absurd, but she waited for the introduction and didn't seem to mind.

So that was one rule. I think another rule was that I had to be home at a reasonable hour. I didn't mind this one at all. In fact, it was quite useful to me. At parties, or if someone had invited us to dinner, I could say quite truthfully, "I have to go home now because of my cat." Suki would be waiting, perched on the back of the sofa like a parrot. She was never cross or reproachful, just glad I was back; and I was glad she was there to greet me. For a cat with temperament she was surprisingly good-natured in a great many ways.

I've just realized what another rule was: she was never to be forced to do anything, she must always be asked. I broke this one sometimes, I confess, though not often, I hope. I wish I hadn't broken it at all. If I had asked for permission to go away for a few weeks, e.g. to visit my mother in India, I'm not altogether certain Suki would have given it to me. And so sometimes I didn't ask, I just went. Suki hated the sight of suitcases. And then there was the matter of the vet. It took a long time to persuade Suki to get into her basket (it was an old picnic basket) so that I could take her to the vet. And sometimes – I admit it – I just picked her up bodily and put her in the basket.

The trips to the vet were quite frequent. The thing was Suki was losing her fur. Two or three vets gave up on it. "It's just something that happens to lilac Burmese," they said. But then a very determined vet took the matter in hand. A long course of injections ensued. The fur grew back, but Suki put on weight. I suppose they would have called it a side effect, but side effects are just effects that they don't want you to notice. They're as effective as any other effects.

Had I consulted Suki she might have said, "No, no injections. I'm content to be a bald cat." Perhaps I did the wrong thing. And was it for her sake or mine? It's just that she hated going to the vet so much, that she wasn't rational about it. And as for the gain in weight, perhaps I should have given her less to eat, forced – encouraged? – her to exercise more? 'Whatever I did, I did for your own good' – it's what parents say to children, though sometimes the children have bitter memories. I suppose, like so much else, some of it's true and some of it's lies, and much of it is a fog of helpless stupidity.

4

A Moral Animal

One day I said to Suki, probably Leaf 2,662, "Suki, are you a socialized being?" It was late in February, we were sitting indoors, the central heating was on and the sun was shining.

I don't think Suki understood what I meant, though what I meant, of course, was had she been socialized into human society. Anyway, I wanted to see what she'd say.

She looked surprised. "Do you mean do I have good manners? Of course, I have excellent manners. I'm charming to your friends when they come to dinner."

That was true. She greeted my friends nicely, let them stroke her if they wished to and was, on the whole, polite and friendly.

"That's right," Suki put in, reading my thoughts, "and

I never interrupt when people are talking. I let them get on with their dinner while I have mine. And I never beg for food, as I understand various members of various species are sometimes prone to do."

"But Suki," I said, "you have your own dinner plate. And if there's anything delicious going, you always have some."

"Yes," agreed Suki. "And anyway, you have nice manners too. You always greet me when I enter a room."

I remembered that as a child I was trained to get up and greet my grandparents whenever they walked in. Was that the same thing? I greeted Suki because I was happy to see her – as I was happy to see them. I nodded at Suki to acknowledge the compliment though I thought it was undeserved.

"Anyway," Suki said suddenly, "I've eaten rarer and more delicious food than you have. That proves I'm more sophisticated than you."

"You're talking nonsense."

"Have you eaten caviar?"

"Yes, that lumpfish stuff. Don't you remember? I gave you some."

"I've had the real thing – Russian caviar."

"How? When?"

"When you parked me with Estelle because you were off on one of your interminable trips. Her brother used to bring it for her from Russia, and she always shared it with us."

"Who is 'us'?"

"The resident cats and me."

"I see. Well, that doesn't prove anything."

"Yes, it does. It proves I'm socialized, not to say sophisticated; and though you won't take me with you on long trips, I have been here and there and am not untravelled or unversed in the ways of the world."

"Suki! You're ridiculous!"

That annoyed her and she was about to go away and sulk, but there was something else I wanted to ask her, so I apologized, "I'm sorry. I only said that because I was envious."

"That's all right," Suki said. "If you had been there, I'd have given you some."

It occurred to me that was true. She probably would have.

"Suki," I said to her earnestly, "do you think you are a very good cat?"

"I'm an excellent cat," Suki replied promptly. "And you're an excellent person. What is the problem?"

I didn't know what to say. Finally I said, "Are there any cats or people who you think are not excellent?"

She considered. "I don't know. After all, I don't go around examining cats and people and deciding whether they are excellent or not."

I wasn't getting anywhere. So I said, "Suki are there any cats or any people you dislike?"

"Oh yes," she answered. "There are some cats and

some people I dislike some of the time. Sometimes I don't even like you very much."

Instead of getting sidetracked and asking, 'Why not?' I managed to persist with my own train of thought. "These cats and people – excluding me – whom you dislike some of the time, do you dislike them because they are not excellent?"

"No," Suki replied, yawning at me, albeit in a fairly polite fashion. "I dislike them because they've annoyed me."

It was clear I was beginning to bore her so I brought out my question all at once. "Suki," I demanded, "are you a moral animal?"

"Do you mean human morality?" she murmured. She looked as though she was nearly asleep by now.

"What other kind is there?"

"I don't know," Suki answered sleepily. "But from what I understand of what you understand of human morality, no, I am not a moral animal."

"But don't you care about being a moral animal?" I yelped at her. I was genuinely shocked.

This time Suki didn't answer. She was genuinely fast asleep.

I let the matter drop. There was no point in waking her up just in order to discuss morality. But I was beginning to suspect that Suki didn't have much use for what she thought of as the human obsession with morality. I wanted to know why. And one day she told me. It was early in September – Leaf No. something or the other. I was sitting at my desk trying to write. She was sitting on top of the desk, in fact, she was sitting on top of my scribbling pad, and in a good-humoured way she was trying to make me give up the struggle (to write immortal verse) and come out into the garden instead.

"I think you're absurd," she said, continuing to sit on top of my scribbling pad.

"Why?" I demanded.

"Being so obsessed with morality and writing all these fables that are so concerned with justice and injustice."

"There are worse obsessions," I said stiffly.

"Oh, I don't mind your obsessions – they occupy you – it's just the way you think about these things that's so silly."

Now that was really insulting, but I wanted to know what she meant, so I decided not to be insulted and asked her what she meant.

"Well, your notion of justice for instance," replied Suki carelessly. "It seems to be a matter of obeying a given set of rules, but if the set-up within which the rules must be obeyed is unfair in the first place, then wherein lies justice?"

I was lost. "What do you mean?" I repeated.

"Well, everybody has a certain amount of property,

say. By 'everybody' I mean every human body. Well, the rules say you mustn't take away someone else's property. But if everyone doesn't have the same amount of property to start with, then how is that fair?"

"Oh, I see," I said in a superior fashion, "you're a socialist or a communist of some sort."

"Nonsense!" Suki retorted. "Card-carrying cats don't exist."

"Well," I said, "let's assume that human justice is imperfect. What do you have against the human quest for morality?"

"I dislike it," Suki said very clearly, "because it's so self-absorbed and self-glorifying."

I was beginning to feel more and more cross, but I wanted to know what she really thought, so I repeated my 'What do you mean?'

"Oh you know," she said yawning at me, as though it was something so self-evident, it hardly needed explaining, "the usual scenario: man at the centre pitted against the rest of creation trying heroically to save his soul. Though what he or she – they generally mean 'he' – is usually trying to save is his own skin."

"What's wrong with that?" I asked. I thought it was a reasonable question.

"Human beings," replied Suki now sounding thoroughly bored and preparing to go into the garden on her own, "human beings are only another species."

"Oh, all that Animal Rights stuff," I said nastily, hoping by my manner to deliver a snub.

"Why not?" replied Suki, "I am, after all, an animal."

That evening I thought we wouldn't be on speaking terms, but when she came in from the garden she seemed to have forgotten about any disagreement we might have had. She found me watching the news on television, jumped onto my lap and quite clearly expected to be brushed and cuddled, and this I duly did.

That night as I was about to fall asleep and she was curled up on the blanket, I asked her suddenly, "All right then, what is the feline notion of a moral universe?" I was hoping to catch her off guard.

"Haven't the faintest," she murmured sleepily.

But I wasn't going to let her off that easily. "No, go on. Off the top of your head. Just what you think."

"Okay," said Suki. "I don't know about a universe, but I think I could live morally in a world in which I didn't have to eat anyone and I didn't get eaten."

"Is that all?" I asked, disappointed.

"It would be something," Suki replied, and she might have said something more, but I interrupted her.

"Anyway cats don't get eaten, so half your battle's won."

"The Chinese eat cats," Suki replied. "And anyway, cats get enslaved and turned into pets."

I was really shocked by her saying this. "That's awful," I said.

"Yes," she agreed, "it is." Then she relented, "Though some forms of servitude are sometimes quite agreeable."

"Suki, you don't serve me!"

"Yes. I do," she replied. "I scare away the mice merely by existing. And anyway, I'm highly ornamental."

"Well, what about me? I serve you too. What about the hundreds of chickens I've boned for you?"

"Perhaps, you're right," Suki conceded. "Perhaps what we have is a partnership, but it's hardly moral."

"You mean because of the chickens?"

"Yes."

"But at least we're moral in relation to each other. I mean we're nice to each other – well, usually. And we do things for each other. Isn't that moral?"

"No," replied Suki. "You're desperate to be moral, aren't you? That's not morality."

"What is it then? Are you saying it's necessity?"

"No," said Suki. "You know perfectly well it's just affection."

"So you're saying that human beings are not particularly capable of morality, but they are capable of love?"

"Something like that. But I'm not particularly interested in human beings."

"Then what are you interested in?"

"Galactic Life."

"What?"

"Galactic Life. I'll tell you tomorrow."

And astonishingly, she did tell me the next morning what she meant.

5

The Spaceship

As usual I was sitting at my desk trying to write. I had got up, I had sat down. I had drunk three cups of tea. All that was normal. Suki was perched on the windowsill looking out at the last of the roses. I never told her so, but I've always loved the way the light fell on her. Sometimes the colour of the cropped fields was exactly like the colour of her fur. She blinked at me from the windowsill in an amiable fashion.

I frowned back at her. "Suki," I grumbled, "you don't really care about my writing at all, do you?"

She bent her head and licked her right paw, then she licked her left paw. "I quite like it," she said, "but sometimes I have to make a terrible effort to accept its assumptions…"

"What do you mean?" I demanded.

"Well, it's so – so –" and suddenly her eyes brightened as she found the right word. "So terribly humanist!" she concluded in triumph.

I was startled. "But Suki," I protested, "that's not necessarily a bad thing."

"Ummm." She turned away and began staring at the roses again. "It is," she murmured with her back to me, "if one has a more dispersed view of the universe."

"Oh? And what is 'a more dispersed view of the universe'?" I mocked her.

"Man (and women) not at the centre," she said tersely.

"Go on," I prodded.

"Well," she replied, deigning to turn around, "Darwin got it half right. We're all related. Put a number of creatures in a pool of time, set time in motion and what you're bound to get is change. But change isn't necessarily evolution, you know. After all, all that can be said about those who survive is that they do survive. Sometimes merely by chance. And if not by chance, then through sheer bloody-mindedness which is hardly commendable."

"So you're saying that the roses you were staring at and the chicken you ate this morning are as important as you?"

"In theory, yes. Of course, in practice, from my own point of view I'm supremely important."

"So what's wrong with my writing?"

"Well, in your writing you are supremely important."

"So are you Suki."

"Yes, but when you write about cats and dogs and blue donkeys, people think you are really writing about them."

"Well?"

"Well, when you write about me, I don't want people to think you're writing about them. I want them to know you're writing about me."

"I think they do know," I said gently.

"Yes, well, I'm the exception. Usually when you write about cats and monkeys and donkeys etcetera, people think you are writing about them."

"Well, would you prefer it if I wrote about people and cats thought I was writing about them?"

"I think it would be better if cats wrote about cats, though cats aren't particularly interested in writing books, and anyway they don't have the money to buy any books."

"Suki," I demanded, "why are you going on about cats when you don't even like your fellow cats?"

"Well, why are you going on about people when you don't even like your fellow people?"

"I'm not."

"You are."

"I'm not."

Suki prepared to jump off the windowsill and I said hastily, "Oh, all right, Suki. If you were writing a story how would you begin it?"

"A story about whom?" asked Suki cannily.

"About you and me," I temporized.

"Well."

"Hah! You wouldn't even know how to begin," I jeered.

"Yes, I would," Suki retorted. "Sit down. I'll dictate and you type it into the computer."

She cleared her throat. "Once upon a time there was a charming entity called Suki and another entity called S, who was also charming, but not quite as charming as Suki."

"Why are we being called 'entities'?"

"To avoid discrimination. Do be quiet."

"Why have you made me less charming than you?"

"Do you think you are equally charming?"

"What's that got to do with it?"

"Oh, all right. Once upon a time there were two equally charming entities called Suki and S who were engaged on a voyage of discovery aboard a spaceship."

"Why a spaceship?"

"To avoid cultural contamination."

"What did the inside of the spaceship look like?"

"Like Devon."

"Don't be silly."

"I'm not being silly. The spaceship was very high

tech and practically any kind of virtual reality could be set up inside it."

"And I suppose the cockpit of this spaceship looked like this cottage?"

"Exactly."

"And the pilot and co-pilot, namely you and me, sat in a space that looked like this study?"

"Not quite," Suki told me seriously. "The computer was geared to my thought waves, and it was green. I prefer green computers to black ones. And there was a swing in there for you to sit on and amuse yourself while I made notes on the strange things we were seeing."

"Er, on this voyage, Suki, were they exploring at random or were they looking for something specific?"

"They were looking for something specific."

"What?"

"Justice."

"But, Suki, I thought you didn't believe in justice?"

"Oh, it would be nice if we could find it."

"In outer space?"

"Why not? With the denizens of outer space we could at least begin with a clean slate."

"Meaning?"

"Well, Darwin made it clear that on earth we're all of us related. But presumably that wouldn't be true of extraterrestrial species."

"But Suki, if we can't even get on with our own

relatives, surely it wouldn't make sense to try to get on with foreign species?"

"And so?"

"And so justice begins at home, don't you think?"

"There!" cried Suki, "That's it in a nutshell! You've got it! That's the kernel of my story. Suki and S go off in a spaceship in quest of justice and in the course of the voyage S understands at last that justice begins at home. Now you can fill in the bits."

"But Suki when we get back do you turn into a vegetarian?"

"Of course not. I'd probably die if I did."

"Well, do I start being nice to the cats next door?"

"No! They're not very nice."

"Then how do we start behaving more justly?"

"I don't know," replied Suki. "I was just telling you how I'd write a story."

I didn't know what to say. "What about poems?" I asked.

"Oh poems are different," Suki said carelessly. "Your fables are often about justice, so your fables are different from mine. But the poems would probably be the same."

"What do you mean?" I asked, feeling slightly stupid – she seemed so sure of herself.

"Poems are about time," she said blinking at me out of her great golden eyes. "Poems are about living and dying. And for any living creature that probably is much the same."

And now Suki's gone and the fact of her dying troubles me.

If when she was alive I could talk with Suki or we could work out – more or less accurately – what the other was thinking, then why can't I speak to her now? Why can't I write a letter in time rather than in space so that I can tell her what I was thinking this afternoon as I did my yogic exercises?

She used to climb into my lap sometimes as I sat cross-legged and did the deep breathing. 'Sooks, you always disliked it when I did the rapid breathing, which required me to jerk my stomach muscles. I think you felt that this kind of thing couldn't possibly be good for me. No matter how many times you saw me do the exercises, you always looked alarmed. But you liked the slow breathing. I've never seen a statue of the Buddha with a small cat curled in his lap, but it's easy to imagine. The Buddha sits as still as a rock – no, I don't mean me – and a small cat sits in his lap. Unlike the Buddha, the cat isn't meditating, she's fast asleep. There would be nothing wrong with that. Surely you would sleep in the Buddha's lap as naturally as the birds sleep in trees.

'I am going to write you a letter. Perhaps it will glide in space-time, and find a point where you and I can exist concurrently if only for a moment and the letter will be a bit of thought or a string of particles of the kind physicists invent, making its way between me and you.'

6

Darwin

Dear Pook,

I've been reading Darwin, and want to tell you about it. I hope you don't object to being addressed as Pook, Sooks, Dingbat etcetera? Anyway Pook is probably quite exalted. Gill used to call you Suki the Pook. I'm not sure what it meant, probably a powerful and mysterious entity who lives in the woods.

Re: Darwin. He says we're related. Surely this ought to have implications. When they say 'All men are brothers,' I suppose they mean each man should love every other man as though that man were his own brother. Madly sexist, but aside from that I don't think they do – I mean love their own brothers or every other man. I think the implications are that if you and I are related, then you ought to be able to share in some or even all of my rights – I mean legal rights, property rights, human rights that sort of thing. But of course, you're gone, so that's irrelevant. All right, you ought to be able to share my status. Not that it amounts to much – but such as it is, it's yours. Or is it?

When the vet said, "Now she must be put out of her misery," I agreed. Would I have done so if you had been a human being? Would I have fought harder? Suki, you hadn't eaten or drunk for four days. You were in the vet's surgery. I brought you home. I had to try to force water down your throat. I took you back. The saline solution kept you going. You were getting weaker and weaker. The vet said you had diabetes. I told him I would inject you every day. It meant nothing. You kept getting weaker. But when he gave you that lethal injection – I had put my hand under your head – futile gesture – you protested, and then you died. I would say, 'God forgive me,' but I don't know if there is a God. I would ask your forgiveness, but why should you forgive me?

I should have taken better care of you, realized earlier that you were ill. That day – a few months earlier – when you shouted at me, I should have known what to do. But Suki, I didn't know what to do. I took you to the vet's – they did this, they did that. I wonder if they knew what they were doing. You have been robbed, and I have been robbed too – though not of my life just as yet. Only a fiend could have invented such a cruel system, a system in which we are given life and then we're robbed. Therefore God does not exist. Call this the emotional proof for the non-existence of God.

This letter goes into the darkness. There must be some way of talking with you.

Here's a strange idea, Pook: Human beings understand that we're all related, and that other species do, in fact, think. They also understand that 'thought' is a natural phenomenon, and they try to make machines that will think. Then they give up on that and go in for biology. What the steel machines do is record and broadcast and what the biological machines do is think. Sounds good – all the species speak to one another. Oh they still kill one another – human beings do that – but at least they speak. There's a problem here though. If you were sitting here, you'd yawn politely and point it out to me. You would say, knowing my species as you do, you strongly suspect that the thought machines would be Mind Slaves and probably members of other species.

Regarding *The Origin of Species*. He does seem to suggest that the march of evolution is ever upward and onward. Nevertheless he sees imperfections – and these he says lend credibility to his theory. Why would the Creator have created imperfections?

Another thing he says could mean that human beings will not go on forever. I suppose that's a good thing – if one takes 'a more dispersed view of the universe'. He says: "And of the species now living very few will transmit

progeny of any kind to a far distant futurity; for the
manner in which all organic beings are grouped, shows
that the greater number of species of each genus, and all
the species of many genera, have left no descendants, but
have become utterly extinct."

As you know, I find what goes on pretty depressing,
but Darwin's concluding sentences are rhapsodic. He
says: "Thus, from the war of nature, from famine and
death, the most exalted object which we are capable
of conceiving, namely, the production of the higher
animals, directly follows. There is grandeur in this view
of life, with its several powers, having originally been
breathed into few forms or into one; and that, whilst
this planet has gone cycling on according to the fixed
law of gravity, from so simple a beginning endless forms
most beautiful and wonderful have been, and are being,
evolved."

I don't know, Pook. 'Higher animals' probably
includes you. But do you really think that's the most
exalted object we're capable of conceiving?

What shall I tell you about in a letter? The news? It
said on the news that the powerful nations are telling the
less powerful to follow their example in the matter of
human rights, but not in the matter of arming themselves.
I didn't know whether to applaud or weep. 'Do as I say
in the name of democracy!' Does it interest you? If you
had the vote, would you exercise it?

And then there's the domestic news. The shed has

been converted into a usable workspace. I'm sitting here writing to you. The sun is shining. There's a CD on of Elly Ameling singing. If you were alive, you'd be sitting here or on the veranda – the shed has one – and perhaps making me open the door a dozen times as you wandered in and out.

I would probably ask your opinion of the little vegetable garden I've begun. It has red lettuces in it and green ones. The peas are doing well, as is the chard. You would probably tell me that you disdain vegetables, but you would probably be glad that they were growing. I suppose that's all it means to be alive really – to be able to enjoy things. But I miss you. It would have been good to have been alive together a little longer.

A little longer? If a living thing asks to be allowed to live a little longer, is that greedy? Who's to judge? And if that living thing cannot speak or if its language is unintelligible, then does its plea go unheard? Doesn't make much difference, I suppose. If all the cabbages and lettuces squeaked, "Don't eat me! Don't eat me! Don't chop off my little head!" I don't suppose human beings would just stand around and allow themselves to starve to death. Things just happen.

But if things just happen, would it make sense to live one's life by the pleasure principle or the selfish principle? You know, just do whatever gives one pleasure and is in one's interest. Did you do that, Suki? But you were often so gentle and kind. Often you seemed to be thinking of me and not just of yourself. And yet I never heard you claim that you were a moral cat. I don't claim to be a terribly moral person. But I try not to be frightfully immoral. But you never said you tried not to be frightfully immoral. I think you would have laughed at me and suggested that I go on about morality within the comfort zone and that you too like the comfort zone, but aren't particularly inclined to moralize about anything while you inhabit it. So then that was our life together? S and Suki (and everyone else) living happily in rural Devon and well within the comfort zone? Suki, there were times when it wasn't all that comfortable. There were worries about money. To which you'd reply that if you can't have any money, you'll be damned if you worry about it. Fair enough. And yet, as I write this memoir I realize it was a sheltered life. If horror poured in, it was through the television.

I want to end this letter with something that would amuse you.

I've racked my brains for a day, but haven't come up with anything yet. And today – of the days that were lost to you – is a different sort of day from yesterday. We've had electrical storms. Do you remember the time we had thunderstorms in the night and Gill was afraid you might be afraid, but found us both snoring peacefully, oblivious to whatever was going on in the heavens? But to return to what might make you smile. At first I thought of news items. Suppose I told you that half the world hasn't enough to eat and the other half is suffering from obesity? I don't think that would make you laugh or cry. You would just shrug. Or suppose I told you a joke? That might not make you smile either. You never thought people were a particularly rational species. All right, suppose I told you something stupid I did? Now that would make you smile. You often thought I did ridiculous things. All right then, Pook, I'm becoming more and more absentminded. The other day I left the keys in the garlic. Gill still teases me about it. But that's not the worst of it. I keep making cups of tea. I forget I've just made a cup and make another one, and I keep leaving them around the house. Gill says I left one in the airing cupboard. (I don't think I did…) Now if you were here, you would smile, and then you would say, "Well, if I spot any cups of tea just lying around and seemingly ownerless, I'll come and tell you about them, shall I?"

Why did making me look silly, make you smile Pook? A bit of sadism? I'm convinced that making me say 'please' a thousand times before you took your worming pills was pure devilment on your part. And if you were here and I accused you – and I do accuse you – you would just smile and say that I looked very funny down on my knees begging a small cat to please have her pill, while the small cat pretended she couldn't work out what I was saying. Surely I wasn't saying that I wanted her to swallow that nasty grey pill? It looked unpalatable and probably did the most dreadful things. And so on.

Well, you were ridiculous too sometimes. Do you remember how you used to flatten yourself under the duvet and hope that if you couldn't see me, I couldn't see you either?

Sometimes I see you out of the corner of my eye, but when I look properly, you're never there. Sooks, what if you were to do a Cheshire cat?

"That's very old-fashioned. I don't call it that."

"What do you call it?"

"I call it slipping through time and space at the speed of thought."

"Sooks? Is that you?"

"Of course. Who else would quibble with you over a thing like that?"

"True. You realize, of course, that sometimes people thought we were both a bit odd? Do you remember Ann Brown's daughter who used to come to feed you when we went away for a day or two? Well, she thought it was strange that she was also being paid to watch tv and cuddle you for an hour."

"It is strange to pay someone to watch tv."

She starts looking out of the window and watches the birds eat their peanuts.

7

Analogies

After a while she asks what I'm doing.

"Writing a memoir," I tell her. "Of you." She doesn't seem impressed.

"I think you're just writing another book – the world seen from a cat's perspective – that sort of thing."

"You don't have a cat's perspective! You're an individualist."

"Yes, but that's supposed to be characteristic of cats. I'm very representative. So are you by the way – for the same reason."

"Does it follow then that cats and people are fairly similar? Not much point in a cat's perspective then? Just a matter of labels?"

"Just a matter of reality. You're beginning to sound post-modernist."

"How can I be post-modernist when I don't even know what that means?"

"It's possible. I am X, therefore I know I am X. It doesn't follow. After all, X could be a word in Chinese or Burmese or Marathi for that matter. Anyway, if I can't represent my own species, it's because I've been colonized."

"By whom?" I demand. She's really pushing it.

"You. A representative of the dominant culture."

"I'm hardly that."

"In relation to me you are. There's probably a doctoral dissertation in there."

"You mean —?"

"Yes. *Analogies between the Domestication of Species and the Colonization of Countries.* Just because you were born in India doesn't mean you can't be a colonist. Anyway, why did you never take me to India with you?"

I'm surprised she asks. I didn't know she wanted to go. I thought she just didn't want me to go.

"Quarantine," I reply knowledgeably.

"Rubbish. We could have managed. I wanted to meet your mother, and your grandmother and your sister."

"My mother dislikes cats," I tell her. "As for my grandmother — Pook, she died the year you were born. Besides, she once told me that though she didn't dislike cats, there were so many needy humans that she felt the humans ought to have priority."

"What about your sister?"

"Well, on Tuesdays and Saturdays she might have been nice to you, but on Wednesdays and Mondays she might have forgotten."

"What about Sundays, Thursdays and Fridays?"

"I don't know."

"Don't Indians like cats?"

"The Indians who keep pets, mostly keep dogs – Alsatians usually."

"Good God!"

"Pook? Why are we talking about what Indians might have thought had you happened to meet any?"

"I'm interested in what they think about cats."

"Isn't it enough that I care about you?"

"Of course not! Besides I don't think you're really a cat lover."

"You mean I don't love every single cat at every single moment? That's ridiculous. You're not a cat lover either! Nor a people lover."

"What I think of people doesn't matter. But what people think of me is of supreme importance."

"To whom?"

"Me. People have power."

"So why do you want to know about Indians? After all, we live in England."

"I think it's what you call comparative anthropology."

"Okay. I think it goes like this. Most Indians don't have anything much to do with cats, and do not like or dislike them particularly, except when they come into the kitchen and steal milk at night. Nor do they think they ought to."

"Ought to what?"

"Like them particularly. With the English it's different. Some English are cat lovers; and most English feel that they ought not to."

"Ought not to what?"

"Dislike cats."

"So if one is a cat, it's better to be in England than in India?"

"Probably."

"Are these Indians you've been telling me about cruel to cats?"

"Not especially. They don't go in for cruelty much. They're good at indifference. They just allow things to happen. You see, an Indian, I mean a Hindu Indian, could have been a cat last time around. You know, reincarnation."

"So if this Hindu Indian was a cat last time, wouldn't she have some fellow feeling for cats this time?" Suki asks.

"I don't think we have much fellow feeling for anyone," I reply thoughtfully. "You see, creatures do what they want, and get what they deserve, and that's why they're caught up in the cycle of birth and rebirth."

I'm not sure I've explained it correctly. What have I got myself into? It's only a metaphor, after all. But Suki is persistent.

"So what did this woman do when she was a cat?"

"She must have been a good cat," I reply. "That's why she got promoted to being a woman." I'm in for it now.

"So women are superior to cats?"

"Well, I'm not sure about the exact system of gradation. For instance, according to some people, males are superior to females. I don't agree."

"No. Well, you wouldn't. I don't either. What are you aiming for next time around?" She makes it sound like a shopping spree.

"What I'm supposed to be aiming for is liberation from the cycle of birth and rebirth," I tell her solemnly.

"Really." She sounds so sceptical, I get annoyed.

"Anyway, you're not an Indian cat. So it shouldn't bother you. You're an English cat of Burmese extraction."

"What's Burma like?"

"I don't know. It's supposed to be bad."

"For cats?"

"For everyone who's powerless. Probably includes cats."

"But isn't everywhere bad for anyone who is powerless?"

"Yes."

"Are we powerless?"

"Not altogether."

"Where is our power hidden?"

"In the bank."

"Pook, change of subject." I hesitate, and then I say, "There's something I've been wanting to say to you. I'm sorry for not realizing you were ill earlier. And I'm also sorry for the injections the vet gave you because you were losing your fur. Do you think they might have caused the diabetes?"

"I don't know. How can I know? Was I losing my fur?"

"Yes. I was afraid you would become a bald cat. Afraid that it would upset you. So I was glad when the vet found an answer. And I'm sorry about the injections – I know you hated them."

"So you're apologizing for the injections that were for my own good?"

"Yes."

"Well, why didn't you explain it to me properly?"

"I did, but it sounded like gobbledygook."

"Well, then how did you expect me to understand it?"

For a while we don't say anything at all. Then I begin again.

"Do you want to know what's happened in the neighbourhood since you left?"

"Go on then, tell me."

"There are two new cats next door. The neighbours

have gone away for a day. I'm supposed to let them out for the night and give them their breakfast and lock them in the house, but one of them's missing. I looked for him everywhere. I looked in all the places you liked or might have liked. First I looked under the lilies. I even shouted for him. But, of course, he doesn't come when I call. On the whole we don't speak."

"You sound worried?"

"A bit. He's related to you, after all."

"Related to me?"

"Same species."

"That's stretching it!"

"All the same, I hope he's all right. Did you know that all our friends were frightfully impressed because you always came when I called?"

"I did know. I let them think I was obedient, but I was only being obliging."

"I know. I did my best to be obliging too."

"Yes, you were quite good."

"Pook?"

"Yes?"

"Can't we stall time's arrow and turn it around?"

"No."

8

The Summit of her Ambition

One day I charged Suki with wrongdoing. It wasn't immediately after she had bitten me. At the time I was too busy pretending to Gill it had only been an accident. I pretended so hard, I almost convinced myself. What happened was that I had woken up at about three or four o' clock in the morning and was going downstairs to get myself a cup of tea. Suki was half racing me downstairs and half getting between my ankles. This was something she sometimes did. I had told her often enough that I didn't think this was a good idea in the middle of the night when I was feeling sleepy; but this time she wasn't paying any attention to me and this time she was also taking little bites at my ankles. When we got to the kitchen, she bit me hard, well, hard enough to draw blood. I couldn't understand it. I checked to see if she had food. I checked my ankle and went back to bed.

A couple of days later I found that the ankle had got infected and it took two weeks of soaking it in hot water and disinfectant to get rid of the infection. Gill was cross with Suki for having bitten me; but I explained that she hadn't known what she was doing, that it was the middle of the night and that she had just got excited.

In my heart I wasn't entirely sure. That was why, two years later, when she was basking among the tulips, and I was weeding carefully around her, I said to her suddenly, "Sooks, are you capable of wrongdoing?"

She didn't even hesitate. "Of course not! As long as I live within the precincts of this garden no harm shall befall me, and I shall remain innocent forever and ever."

Sometimes she was too clever for her own good, so I said crossly, "Come on, Sooks, this isn't paradise and you know it."

"Well then why are you asking? Of course, I'm capable of wrongdoing. What are you getting at?"

"Why did you bite me?"

"When?"

"When my ankle got infected."

"Oh that. I don't remember. Probably just for the hell of it."

"But Pook, the infection was quite nasty."

"Well, how was I to know it would get infected? And anyway, it was only a little nip."

"Well, but aren't you in the least bit sorry?"

The Pook considered. "I am a little. But I don't like being harangued and harried."

Having established that she was capable of wrongdoing and of remorse of sorts, i.e. that she had some notion of ethics, a few weeks later I decided to find out where she stood on aesthetics.

It was Leaf No. 3,078 probably. She was sitting on my desk washing herself. I was trying to write and, as happened frequently, getting nowhere.

"Pook," I said to her thoughtfully, "where do you stand on art and literature and all that sort of thing?"

"Do you mean poetry?" she asked warily, preparing to jump off the desk.

"No, oh no. Let's skip poetry," I said quickly. I didn't feel strong enough to bear her true opinion of my work. "No, I mean music for example. That sort of thing."

"I quite like Chinese opera," she told me.

I didn't believe her. "When have you ever heard Chinese opera?"

"I've hear it once or twice on telly. And anyway it was in that film you were watching the other night – 'Farewell my something'."

"Why do you like it?" I demanded.

"Why do you dislike it?" she retorted.

I didn't know what to say, so I changed the subject. "What else do you like that gives you aesthetic satisfaction?"

"What is 'aesthetic satisfaction'?" Suki asked sweetly.

"Er – refined sensual pleasure."

She pondered. "Well, I like a clean dinner bowl. You always do clean the bowl before you give me fresh food. Thank you for doing it."

"It's a pleasure," I replied. "What else?"

"I like the space around my bowl of food and my

bowl of water to be clean. No bits of food, or crumbs or dust. But you always do make sure the floor is clean."

"It's no trouble," I replied. "And anyway, Pook, you're a very fastidious eater." But I didn't know whether being a fastidious eater counted towards aesthetics, so I said to her, "What about visual things? What do you like to look at?"

"Tulips," she replied promptly.

"Why?" I asked.

"Clever shapes, variegated colours and a faint perfume. And I don't like being cross-examined. I'm going into the garden," she snapped at me. She jumped off the desk and stalked off. Over her shoulder she called, "Oh, and I like day lilies. I like sleeping under them."

"Huh," I retorted. "That's probably because you think they make a good backdrop for you and set you off to advantage."

She paused in the doorway just long enough to inform me that she thought she looked good regardless of the backdrop. Very conceited I thought, but I also thought there was some truth in that. Most cats manage to look good no matter what the circumstances. Two seconds later she put her head in through the doorway. "And for your information," she told me, "I like sleeping under the lilies because they offer me a striped shade, which allows me to be hot and cool at the same time." With that she vanished and left me wondering whether a sybarite was the same thing as an aesthete. Close enough, I decided.

The truth was I had got it into my head that I should try to work out just how human Suki was. I didn't tell her about this project. I was afraid she'd say something like being human was hardly the summit of her ambitions. But I persisted with it quietly and every now and then I would ask her what I thought was a perspicacious question.

When she came back in I had another question for her, but she cut me short. "S," she said severely, "you are going through a most peculiar phase. I hope it's only a phase and won't last long. You keep asking me what you think are intelligent questions."

"What's wrong with that?" I said defensively. "I'm just making conversation."

"But you get cross when I don't give you what you consider the right answers."

"I do not."

"Yes, you do."

"No, I — Look, I'll prove it to you. I'll ask you a question and when you answer it, I won't be cross."

"No, but I might be cross," Suki replied. "I don't like being asked intelligent questions."

"Oh, so you do think they're intelligent?"

"No," she snapped. "You think so. Anyway, what's all this about? Is a cat food company paying you to do some market research?"

I hesitated. "Yes, something like that," I told her.

"All right," Suki said, "for every question I answer, you can give me five of the cat biscuits I particularly like."

"But Suki," I wailed, "they're bad for you."

"That's your problem," Suki retorted. "Which do you care about most: my health or your happiness?"

Then she smirked as though she had made a particularly good joke. I didn't know what to do. I had spent some time trying to formulate the next question as I felt it was quite central to my research on Suki's humanity. The question had to do with the extent to which Suki was concerned with status — human or otherwise. I decided that just this once five cat biscuits wouldn't hurt her too much. I also told myself to note somewhere that she seemed to have a degree of financial acumen: she had insisted on the biscuits first and then the answer.

Suki ate her five biscuits in a leisurely manner, took a sip of water, washed herself delicately, but thoroughly, and then suggested we stroll into the garden. Once we were outside, she seated herself on the grass, curled her tail around her, glanced at me, and, in her grandest manner, murmured, "Proceed."

I cleared my throat and asked earnestly, "Suki, does it afford you some satisfaction that you have an astonishing pedigree that many snobs would die for?"

She looked at me out of her great golden eyes as

though she couldn't believe her ears. "Oh S," she cried, "you are unbelievable sometimes!" Then she rolled over and over on the grass and laughed and laughed and swatted my toes until I fell on the grass too and rolled over and over with her.

Then she sat up and looked at me solemnly, "Of course it's of some consequence."

"Why?"

"Because," she said slowly and carefully as though she was explaining something particularly obvious, "there are loads of people to whom it is of consequence, and my pedigree makes them nicer to me than they would have been otherwise."

"And you want people to be nice to you?"

"Of course, don't you?"

9

Renaissance Entity

I had established to my own satisfaction that Suki was at least as human as I was. She understood the difference between good and evil – well, sort of. At least she could talk about it. She was fastidious. She said she liked Chinese opera. She understood the importance of social status. She had a sense of humour – even if it mostly manifested itself in being amused by me, and not when I was intentionally amusing, but by what, I suppose, she would call my 'antics'. And she was capable of wrongdoing – she sometimes bit people. The chief difference between us seemed to be that she was relatively powerless.

One day, I forget which day it was – Leaf No. 3,000 and something – I saw in the papers that someone had done a big research project which established clearly that deer suffered when they were hunted. I told this to Suki. Just once in a while something would happen that left her speechless. This was one of those times. We looked at each other. After a while she murmured, "When they cut me, I bleed."

When Suki was alive I hadn't meant to write at length about her. She did enter the odd poem or fable, and as what I had to say was more or less flattering, she didn't mind. Still, I hoped she would approve of the memoir I was writing. And so one day when she appeared on my desk top in her Cheshire cat manner – so real that she really did seem to be there – I said to her, "If you were to write about yourself, Sooks, what would you say?"

She thought about it before replying, "I wouldn't write about me. I would write about Super Cat."

"Super Cat?"

"Yes, me as I would like me to be. You know, flies through the air, has X-ray vision, is kind to the elderly and bashes up bullies. That sort of thing."

"Elderly?"

"Yes. Like you. Why not?"

"No, seriously, Suki. If you had to write about yourself, what would you say?"

"I was born. I was traumatized. I was loved. I got sick. I died."

"And if you were writing about Super Cat?"

"Oh. Well, that would have to be a split narrative.

Super Cat would have an alternate identity as Suki, an ordinary household cat who lived with an ordinary person called S."

"Do you think I'm terribly ordinary?"

"Sure, why not? You have a few eccentricities, but they're well within the norm."

That wasn't what I had meant. I had been hoping that she might have noticed my exceptional talent. I thought it best not to say anything.

"Why does Super Cat Suki have a dual identity?"

"To give her some respite from the paparazzi."

"Does S know she is Super Cat?"

"Yes, S is the one entity to whom Super Cat has confided her secret."

"Why has Super Cat chosen S?"

"Because S forgives her."

"For what?"

"For being so super."

I was beginning to think that Super Cat was a bit of a pain.

But Suki said, "Super Cat Suki is still Suki, you know. If you miss me so much that you talk to me even when I'm gone, then why not let me be Super Cat sometimes? It's fun."

I relented. "Why is it fun?" I wanted to know.

"Well, Super Cat Suki can do a great many things. She traverses space, has been known to race with comets. And the speed of her thoughts is faster than lightning."

"What does she think about?"

"Of the nature of the universe. The metaphysics of black holes. Of what would happen if anyone or anything ever exceeded the speed of light. And whether to answer that question it's actually necessary to exceed the speed of light or only to have the necessary imagination."

I was a bit overwhelmed in spite of myself. "So Super Cat is a physicist?" I managed at last.

"Sometimes. Super Cat is a Renaissance Entity. She leads a varied and busy life."

I knew I was supposed to ask what Super Cat did, so I did ask, half hoping that Sooks might be at a loss for an answer.

Suki didn't hesitate. "Oh she does all sorts of things. Rescues kittens who've climbed to the topmost branches of tall trees and can't get down, for example."

"How? How does she rescue them?"

"She just picks them up by the scruff of the neck and drifts down gently in slow motion."

"Really! She can defy gravity?"

"Of course. She can levitate and gravitate. And she can fly."

Who was I to pick holes in Suki's fantasy? "What else does she do?" I asked humbly.

"She upholds justice and fights evil."

"And can she tell the difference between the good guys and the bad?"

Suki shrugged. She wasn't going to be drawn. "Mostly she can."

I realized that we had been talking for quite a while now, and for Suki this had been a long conversation.

"Aren't you tired?" I asked.

"I'm tireless," Suki replied.

"How long can you talk?"

"That depends on you. On your powers of concentration to keep me here."

"'As long lives this, and this gives life to thee'?" I murmured.

"Something like that, but not quite so grand."

"Suki, are you immortal?" I demanded.

Sooks smirked. "Sure. Super Cat hardly needs to eat or drink, and does so only to be sociable. For all practical purposes she'll live forever."

"What are practical purposes?" I asked.

"Your purposes," Suki replied at once.

I had a selfish thought, and Suki, of course, heard it at once. It went something like this. "Then I would have you all my life. And when I died, you'd be the one who'd have to mourn."

"Yes," she said gently, and then she did the Cheshire cat thing – she vanished. It seemed to me that where she had been, there was for a moment a black cut-out carved out of space, an absence. I began to think about Suki, and everything I remembered had holes and absences carved in it in the shape of a small cat. The tulips on a spring day had their faces eaten away. The window behind the desk where she used to sit was half gone. The floor had dark patches where she used to be.

And then there was Suki's voice again. I could almost feel her head against my arm. "No, not like that. I didn't take away anything. I filled the days. And you were fortunate. As was I."

PART II
The Vipassana
Trek

10

The Menagerie

Time goes by as it always does and I'm sitting cross legged inside the meditation dome. Suki is sitting near me.

"What are you doing?" she asks.

"Learning to meditate."

"Why?"

"To become detached."

"From what?"

"From all the things that I'm attached to."

"Ah."

I can't quite read the expression in her eyes. Does she really want to know?

"Suki, detachment doesn't mean…" I start again, "According to the Teacher, human beings spend all their time craving for what they don't have, worrying about whether they are going to lose what they do have, and crying over what they once had. So you see, it's better to be detached. That way I'll miss you less."

"But I want to be missed!" she says indignantly.

I'm taken aback. "You do?" I ask.

"Of course," she retorts. "If you went out of a room, wouldn't you want people to notice that you had left?"

I don't know what to say. "Well, I don't suppose I'll succeed," I tell her.

"Aren't you any good at it?"

I feel foolish, but I had better tell the truth.

"No," I reply. "I'm not much good at it. And the menagerie doesn't help. They keep getting in the way."

"What menagerie?" She sounds surprised. "Have you another cat?"

"Of course not. How could I? I would always be cross with her for not being you."

"Well, who's in this menagerie then? Blue donkeys, one-eyed monkeys? That sort of thing?"

"No, no, this lot inside my head. I mean they're part of my head. There's Magsie for instance."

"Magsie?"

"The magpie."

"You have a magpie inside your head?" Suki is frowning.

I try to explain quickly. "Suki, the magpie was the first to appear — right at the start — when I was trying to learn this meditation. She's the retrieval mechanism. She brings straws into my mind – thoughts, memories, objects from the past. Perhaps I'm supposed to spin them into gold, but I don't, of course. They disappear quite quickly."

As I say this the magpie hops forward, looks at Suki doubtfully, and gets ready to take off.

"Are you saying this bird retrieved me?" Suki sounds incredulous.

"You are too heavy," Magsie replies in a carefully neutral voice. "More substantial than a straw. Perhaps the equal of a thousand or even a million straws put together."

Suki doesn't know how to take that. She blinks. An old trick. From that anyone who's watching can gather what they like.

This is getting too heavy for Magsie. She wants to leave. "There are other retrievers," she says hastily, as she makes her excuses. "Chipsie, for example. She's a hoarder."

The magpie leaves. Suki is looking at me in a concerned manner.

"I'm all right," I reassure her. "They were there all the time. Chipsie, Magsie and the rest. The meditation allowed them to emerge."

"You meditated about them and they appeared?" Suki sounds unbelieving.

"No, no. Just the reverse. I was supposed to be

concentrating on the sensations sweeping over my body time after time, but these creatures kept interrupting. That's when I became aware of them. They're perverse."

Just then Chipsie appears. She's a grey chipmunk with brown stripes. She sits back on her haunches, lets her front paws droop and recites: "I can tell you what the sound of one hand clapping is like. It is like the square root of minus one. It isn't possible, but it can be imagined."

Suki stares at her out of her golden eyes. The chipmunk runs away.

"Now look what you've done," I say crossly.

"What was I supposed to do?" retorts Suki. "Applaud?"

"Yes. Why not?" I reply. "Don't you think that was a clever little nugget she had stashed away for future use?"

Suki shrugs, an imperceptible, elegant shrug – the kind she's good at. "If you say so. Who else is in the squat?"

"Are you calling my mind a squat?"

"Well, these outlandish inhabitants…"

"They're not outlandish. They live there. They're native – like the strange life forms at the bottom of the ocean. I don't know what you're complaining about. They are well behaved."

"They are not!" Suki expostulates. "Piling up straws, reciting unasked…" She sounds annoyed.

"All right, I'll call Princie," I say in an effort to placate her.

"Who's Princie?"

"Well, he's a dog. A retriever of sorts. Not pedigreed like you. But he fetches and carries. Does what he's asked."

At the mention of his name, Princie comes bounding in, tries to lick my hand, wags his tail at Suki. Suki barely manages to repress a snarl, but he appears not to notice.

"Oh wow!" he says. "You must be Suki. You have no idea how many items I've fetched and carried to do with you. There's a whole archive devoted to you! Very honoured to make your acquaintance I'm sure." He stretches out his front legs and bows humbly.

Suki is mollified, but she has had enough. "Go away," she says clearly.

"Yes, please go," I add hastily.

Princie leaves at once.

Suki and I face each other.

"I don't think I like meditation," she informs me.

"The Teacher says cats can't meditate, only human beings can."

"Ha! I bet I could meditate if I wanted to. And anyway you can't either."

"I know. Suki, please, help me."

"Help you with what?"

"With everything. With the menagerie. Oh, and with the rats. I need you, Suki."

Suddenly she relents. "I always help you," she says
jauntily. "Tell me about the rats. Are they in your head
too?"

"No, no, they're outside."

"Well, come on then."

"They're quite large," I try to warn her, but she's on
her way out. I follow meekly.

11

Gambolling on the Grass

When we emerge from the meditation dome, the
leaves of the sweet chestnut have turned golden and are
blowing in the wind. Suki blinks in the bright sunlight.
She looks around.

"This isn't where we live," she says. I don't think
she approves. "It's quite nice here, but why don't we go
home? Where are we?"

"At the Meditation Centre. I told you I'm learning
to meditate."

"And you need me to deal with the menagerie in
your head?"

"Well, yes, but also with those." I point across the
lawn at the row of trees.

"Rats!" Suki exclaims. "You want me to fight them?" She sounds enthusiastic.

"Well, no. This is a non-violent place. I thought your presence might be enough."

"You want me to scare them off?"

"That was the idea."

"And you want me to help you meditate?"

"Well, I thought we could try to meditate together."

"Even though the Teacher said cats can't"

"The teacher could be wrong. I thought it might suit you. It's a Burmese meditation."

"What's that got to do with it?"

"Well, you're Burmese," I say lamely.

We're in my room now and Suki sits on the bed washing herself. She doesn't think I deserve an answer.

There's a tap on the door. I don't see anyone. Somebody coughs. I look down and I see a rat on the doorstep carrying a white flag. I want to jump back, but I control myself. Suki has her hackles raised.

"This is ridiculous!" I say to the rat.

"It is not ridiculous," the rat says quietly. "We are intelligent creatures and I need to talk to you." He puts his flag down. "I know I disgust you. I'll stay on the doormat. But I do need to talk – with both of you," he adds, looking at Suki who is still on the bed, her back arched.

"We don't talk to rats," Suki tells him. "We kill them. Aren't you afraid of me? Go away. Do you want to fight?"

"I don't want to fight," the rat replies calmly. "And yes, I am afraid of you. But I do need to talk to you."

It seems unreasonable not to give him a hearing. "All right. Talk. But stay where you are." It's hardly polite, but it's the best I can do.

"Did you know that the rat genome is of a similar size to that of humans?" Rat begins.

I grunt.

"We probably have far more in common with you than you have in common with Suki, for example."

"You do not!" Suki growls.

"Not interested in DNA," I tell him. "Are you done?"

"No, wait." Rat doesn't move. "We're starting a Public Relations campaign to convince people about how nice we are. We thought we'd start here, because here, they refrain from killing us outright."

"You carry diseases!" I retort ferociously.

"Well, so would you if you had to live the way we have to! That's what I'm getting at. Better living conditions."

"Look. I've heard you out. Now would you go away, please. And take your flag with you," I say in as neutral a voice as I can manage. With my right hand I'm stroking Suki to calm her down.

Rat shakes his head sorrowfully. "You really don't like us, do you? But that's because you don't know us. Why not let me move in with you for a day or two? It's cold outside. I could do with the warmth, and you could get to know me. I'm a pleasant fellow. Rational. Knowledgeable. With a good sense of humour. In short, excellent company —"

I interrupt rudely. "What are you really getting at? What do you want?"

"I want," says Ratty, pronouncing each word distinctly, "I want people to substitute Rats for Cats. We are smaller and nicer and —"

Suki springs from the bed and lunges at him. He shoots out of the door and makes for the bushes. But he's persistent. Over his shoulder he calls out to us, "Haven't you seen us gambolling on the lawns? We're charming creatures."

Back inside the room, Suki glares at me. "You brought me here for this?" She's angry.

"No, wait, Suki. I need help with the mouse hole," I say plaintively. She isn't listening. She lashes her tail a couple of times and falls asleep on my bed. I try to catch half an hour's sleep before I have to meditate again. I keep worrying about Suki. I'm not sure she likes it here. I thought perhaps she would and we could have an adventure.

12

The Mouse Hole

When Suki wakes up she's curled up on my lap. I'm sitting inside the meditation Dome. She's purring loudly. "Shush," I whisper in her ear. "We're supposed to be silent."

"It's all right," she whispers back. "They can't hear me. What are we doing here?"

"Watching the mouse hole," I whisper to her.

"Don't whisper," Suki instructs me. "They can hear you, and they'll think that you're either mad or bad. Just think at me. What mouse hole?"

"The metaphorical mouse hole I'm supposed to be watching with the alertness, awareness and concentration of a cat, and with equanimity, of course."

"You mean, you imagine a mouse hole and then

you watch it in the hope that an imaginary mouse will appear?"

"No! I'm supposed to be aware of the sensations rising and disappearing all over my body, but only if they're actually there. I'm not supposed to imagine anything."

"But you want me to teach you to catch an imaginary mouse?" I don't know if Suki is genuinely puzzled or if she's teasing me.

"Suki, the mouse is only a sensation, and the vipassana mouse is only there sometimes. Oh, and I'm supposed to be aware that it's ephemeral."

"I see." (I don't think she sees at all.) "Well, what's stopping you?"

"The Babbler."

"Who's The Babbler?"

"He's a nondescript brown bird. He talks a lot. Shall I introduce you?"

"Is this another one of the creatures inside your head?"

"Well, yes."

"What's his function?"

"One of his functions is to inflate Toadie."

"And what does Toadie do?"

"He inflates and deflates."

"Whew!" Suki shakes her head. I think that if she weren't such a nice-natured cat, she'd jump off my lap, run outside and zap a few rats.

She condescends to be introduced to The Babbler. It can't be said he's lurking in the wings. He likes to be centrestage. As we approach he's babbling.

Suki looks up at him. "What's he babbling about?" she asks puzzled.

I listen carefully. "Something about being the teacher's favourite perhaps, and about being such a sweetie and trying so hard and being Indian and knowing how to do a namaskar properly."

Suki looks at him aghast and is about to turn away, when I say, "No, wait. He's not so bad really. Just full of hot air. What they call aspiration. You know – what he'll do. Who he'll become. What people will say."

"You mean he lives in the future?" asks Suki. She looks at him doubtfully. He's very puffed up and about ten times her size.

"I construct things," the Babbler tells her, looking down at her over his puffed-out chest. "Magsie brings straws and I make castles out of them."

When Suki doesn't reply, he continues defensively. "Well, why shouldn't I? Somebody has to."

He continues babbling. "I'll send my friend that photo I took of the hen pheasant. Then she will think I'm a sweetie – and clever."

Suki looks puzzled. We continue listening.

"We could go on the train to Southampton. Then take a taxi to the docks. The taxi driver will know the way to the docks."

Babbler becomes aware of us listening and becomes defensive. "Well, somebody has to make plans, you know. I mean, map out the future before it happens. And anyway, I can be as cogent and coherent as anybody. Listen!"

He recites: "*Once we are outside the dome, we breathe in gulps of air. There are clouds scudding overhead and a wind ruffling the trees.*"

"Shall I give that to the kingfisher or to the chipmunk?" he asks.

When I don't answer immediately, he turns away.

"Who's the kingfisher?" Suki wants to know.

"Oh, she's beautiful. Looks as though she's made of metal. And very Byzantine — you know, as though set upon a golden bough to sing."

"And she sings?"

"Well, no. She's another retriever. Sometimes the magpie retrieves a straw that glitters so brightly that it looks as though it has already been transmuted into gold. Kingsie dives for it and works it with her beak until she is satisfied."

"And then?" asks Suki, interested in spite of herself.

"Then she gives it to the chipmunk. Would you like to meet her?"

But Suki has had enough. "You should either be concentrating on the metaphorical mouse hole," she says severely, "or we should go outside." She pauses. "How do the Babbler's stories usually go?" she asks curiously.

"They go something like this," I reply. "Such-and-such will happen. Then So-and-so will say or do such-and-such. Then I will say or do such-and-such. And then I will look GLORIOUS!"

Suki looks at me. For once she's speechless.

I try 'watching the mouse hole' for a bit, I mean being aware of the sensations rising and disappearing, rising and disappearing, but Suki keeps digging her claws into my shoulder. I think she's trying to generate sensations so that I can be aware of them. It's distracting.

"Okay," I say to her. "I'm getting very stiff. Let's go outside for a few minutes so that I can stretch my legs."

Once we are outside the dome, we breathe in gulps of air. There are clouds scudding overhead and a wind ruffling the trees.

"Suki," I say to her, "it's not so bad here. We could have an adventure."

"Inside your head?"

"Well, half inside, half outside. 'Mind has mountains; cliffs of fall/ Frightful, sheer…'"

She looks interested. "A trek?" she asks.

"Sort of," I mumble.

13

Fleas

"Let's sit on that bench over there," Suki says to me.

"Can't," I tell her. "I have to go back into the dome."

"Don't you get a break?"

"Well, to eat and to sleep and to bathe. We're supposed to watch the mouse hole twelve hours a day – that includes an hour of listening to the teacher."

"Sounds tough. Is the Teacher hard on you?"

"No, he's kind. He wants to help."

"Help you do what? Catch mice?"

"Suki!"

"Okay, okay. Well, you'd better deal with my problem. I've got fleas."

"How can you have fleas when you're a —"

"I know, a cat spirit. Well, they're flea spirits then. Anyway, I need to be brushed and they need to be combed out of my fur."

"Suki, I haven't got a brush, and I'm not allowed to leave this place till the ten days are over. You know that."

"You could use yours."

"You want me to use my comb and brush to comb out your fleas?"

"I'd let you use mine. Besides, they're only flea spirits."

As she turns her head away I realize she's laughing at me. Nevertheless, she insists that she needs to be brushed. I ask the person-in-charge for a hairbrush, she gives it to me with a smile.

We settle on my bed and I start brushing Suki.

"Suki, what do you like best?"

"Being cuddled."

"Next?"

"Being brushed."

"Next?"

"Being warm."

"Next?"

"Food – provided it's good food. Salmon or something."

"What about me?"

"Oh, I like sitting on your lap and being brushed best of all."

For her, it's all unproblematic, I think gloomily.

Suki overhears. "Of course, it's unproblematic. Why shouldn't it be?"

Suddenly The Babbler interrupts. "I solve problems, you know. I think hard and look into the future and MAKE PLANS. I don't know why you make such a fuss about Kingsie and Magsie. They're mechanical birds. The magpie just retrieves straws at random. I have to make do with whatever I get. As for the kingfisher – it's obvious she's got a magnet attached or a homing mechanism. She zeroes in on glittering straws and snaps them up. Probably thinks they're fish! Whereas I think things –"

I don't dare interrupt. The Babbler's in full swing and about to go on about his other merits, but Suki has had enough. "SHUT UP!" she shouts at him. The Babbler retreats, shrinks and disappears.

Suki jumps off the bed. "I'm going for a walk," she flings at me.

"I'll come," I offer.

"No thanks," she retorts. "You've got your menagerie to look after. You'd better go into the dome and tend to them."

"But Suki, I'm not supposed to deal with them in the dome," I wail.

"That's your problem." She stalks out, leaving the door wide open.

I shut it hastily in case Ratsie appears.

Then I open it again and go back into the dome. I try to concentrate on sensations rising and falling, rising and falling. "Why would anyone in their right mind do that?" That must be The Babbler. "Shut up, Babbler." Damnation! I had forgotten. This is one of the hours when we have to do the Meditation of Great Determination. We mustn't uncross our legs, we mustn't fidget, and we mustn't squirm. Good thing Suki isn't here. She'd probably distract me. Just then Suki snuggles into the blanket I've wrapped around myself. She smells of fresh air and autumn leaves. Suddenly I remember how Suki used to jump into my lap when I did the breathing exercises during my yoga sessions. The magpie must have brought that straw. Sometimes she brings good straws.

"Suki, do you remember?"

"Of course, I remember. You used to breathe fast in a very strange way. Almost like panting. It made me worry."

"That was how I was supposed to do the exercise. Suki, do you suppose we looked quite sweet? I mean a small person with a small cat in her lap sitting cross-legged in front of a giant image of the Buddha?"

"There was no giant image."

"No, but we could imagine one."

"You really suppose that the Buddha is diddled just by our looking sweet?" She sounds sceptical, brisk and scornful. Then she relents, "He's probably nice to everyone."

*Buddham sharanam gacchami… I take refuge in the
Buddha. I take refuge…*

I try again. "Those were good days, Suki. I miss
you."

"Well, I miss you too." Suddenly she's impatient. "But
what's the good of that?" She starts to walk away, comes
back and perches on my shoulder. "Ha! When I left your
room I went into the shrubbery and chased the rats. At
least they're real."

"Are you saying The Babbler isn't real? He's very real
I assure you."

"Well, whatever. These are more real and I had a go
at them."

"You hunted the real rats?"

"Yes, I nearly got a couple of them, until Ratsie
appeared with his stupid white flag."

"And then what happened?"

"Oh well, I told him what was what. His idea of
substituting rats for cats was pure rubbish, and wasn't just
a matter of changing one letter of the alphabet. Cats are
superior to rats as ordained by God, nature, whoever."

"What did Ratsie say?"

"You're on first name terms?"

"Suki! You called him Ratsie. What did he say?"

"He said I wasn't being reasonable. He proposed a
contest in order to establish that rats were as good as cats
if not better."

"And you accepted?"

"What was I supposed to do? I couldn't turn down a challenge. I was pretty sure I could beat him in an honest to goodness fight even if he was almost as big as me and a lot younger."

"So you fought? Suki!"

"What are you complaining about? I thought you brought me here to deal with the rats? Anyway, we didn't fight. He produced a chess board."

"Who won?"

Suki hesitates. She says reluctantly. "Well, he was winning. He must have practised. So I knocked over the chess board and zapped him."

"You hurt him?"

"Well, no, he escaped." She snuffles into the blanket and goes to sleep.

I can hear the Teacher's voice. *Bhavatu sabba mangalam, bhavatu sabba ... May all things be well...* The hour of Great Determination is up. My right leg hurts. I'll have to uncross my legs carefully and get up very slowly in case I topple over. At least I've got through it, and between Suki and The Babbler I was distracted and the pain wasn't too bad. But I wasn't supposed to be distracted.

"It was all your fault, Suki," I tell her, knowing I'm being unfair.

"Yes, me and The Babbler, we distracted you," she agrees.

"I don't cooperate with The Babbler!" I protest.

"No?" She's insouciant.

She changes the subject. "Anyway, I think you loved me because I was so unproblematic," she throws at me cheerfully.

Preposterous! "You unproblematic?! What about all the problems that meant going to the vet? What about the cats next door? What about the time you had some catmint?"

"That catmint was your fault. Your friend brought it for me. But on the whole these were all problems you could solve. Your problem with your own species is that they present you with problems you can't solve."

She looks very pleased with herself.

14

An Indian Story

I wake up well before four o'clock the next morning.
No need for the gong or the alarm clock. Suki's perched
on my pillow waiting for me to open my eyes. "Come
on," she says. "There's starlight outside."

I scramble into my clothes. "What about the rats?" I
whisper.

"Oh, don't worry about the rats. They're fast asleep.
And anyway, I'll protect you. Come on."

It's still dark outside. It is a starlit night, no, morning.
Some clouds. They're moving past slowly. I like the skies
here. Soon, a little bit of light will start colouring the air.

"Come on," says Suki. "Let's go into the woods."

"But Suki I can't see. It's dark in there. No lights.
Besides, I have to be in the meditation dome by 4:30."

"I can see. I'll get you back. Oh, do come!"

I stumble along behind her. As we walk over the grass on the way to the trees, I trip over a molehill. Suki waits. I recover my balance and we enter the trees, mostly silver birch and beech. I can see a little bit now, and Suki is good about waiting for me. I don't feel nervous anymore. The beech leaves have turned into copper. They look metallic in the early light. And many of the silver birches still have their leaves. When a breeze goes by they seem to straighten themselves and make their leaves quiver like castanets. I feel happy.

"Come on," I say to Suki, "we have to go back. It's nearly 4:30."

Suki turns back reluctantly. I trip over a different molehill and this time I fall on my face.

"That was fun," Suki says.

I assume she means going into the woods.

I pick myself up. "Yes, it was," I agree.

Inside the dome I wrap my blanket around me and sit down to meditate. Suki curls up on my lap and falls asleep. It's astonishing how much she can sleep.

I try to meditate. Try to watch the breathing first. That's right. Now the sensations. From the top of my head to the tip of my toes. From the tip of my toes to the top of my head. I wonder why we didn't encounter any rats just now. Do they really sleep at night? Just like people? Perhaps these rats do, as they're free to gambol on the lawns when the sun shines. No person would dare harm them. Did Ratsie really challenge Suki to a game of chess? Suddenly it occurs to me that Suki made up the whole thing.

"Suki!" I say to her, stroking her head to wake her up. "Did you make it up?"

"Make what up?" she asks drowsily.

"Your foray into Rat Territory."

"Let me think. Oh yes, I did make it up. I thought you'd enjoy it. It's just the sort of thing you'd have made up about me."

"Well, if you didn't attack the rats, what did you do?"

"I went back to your room and fell asleep. Telling you that Ratsie was about to beat me at chess was a nice touch, wasn't it? He wouldn't have beaten me really."

"I see."

"You're supposed to be meditating. I want to sleep."

"Suki, would you like it if I cared about you less?"

"Of course not. Don't be silly. And do let me sleep."

"It's not silly, Suki. It's crucial. I didn't phrase it correctly. I mean if I wasn't so attached to you. If I was happy to let you be."

"Well, on the whole you do let me be."

"But all you want to do is sleep."

"What's wrong with that? We cats are so energetic, we need lots of sleep."

"Suki, perhaps the Teacher's right when he says birds and beasts and rats and cats aren't capable of meditation. Only human beings are."

"Well, you don't seem to be doing too well yourself. And anyway, I though he said I was good at watching the mouse hole."

"Yes, Suki, but would you be able to watch the mouse hole with detachment and equanimity if there wasn't a mouse in it?"

"What, not even a metaphorical mouse?"

I decide she's making fun of me so I don't say anything. After a short pause she says. "You mustn't think I wouldn't make a foray into rat land. I'm up for it. It's just that I fell asleep."

"And I'd join you in the foray, but it's against the rules. No violence against our fellow creatures."

"They're not my fellow creatures!"

"Well, they think they are."

"Ok. Well, if you can't meditate, and won't let me sleep, let's go for a walk."

"I can't, Suki. I'm supposed to sit here and try."

"Are you trying?"

"Sort of."

"Well, if you can't manage, you can tell me a story. I'll half doze and half listen to it."

"About what?"

"About a cat."

"I can't recollect any stories about cats right now. I'll tell you one about a king."

"Is this an Indian story?"

"Yes."

"Oh well, I know how it goes. Once upon a time there was a king who went to the forest, sat down under a tree and meditated hard."

"That's right. Well, unlike me, this king was really good at meditating, so that by the end of his life he was ready to be liberated from the endless cycle of birth and re-birth. As he was dying he saw a doe with a fawn, and then he saw the doe being killed by an arrow. His dying thought was concern for the fawn. What would happen to the poor thing now?"

"Sounds like a nice chap?"

"Well, maybe, but that was his undoing. All his meditation and detachment came to nothing. He wasn't liberated from the cycle of birth and rebirth at all. In his next life he was born as a deer so that he could look after the fawn."

"Oh." I don't think Suki knows what to make of this. I don't either really. I wait.

At last she says, "Do you believe in all this? I mean birth and re-birth and reincarnation?"

I pounce on that. "Suki! You know that literal belief is a waste of time. We should think of it as a Meaningful Metaphor."

"Like the mouse hole with the mouse which isn't in it?"

"Well, yes."

"Well, who will you be next time around?"

"No, let's talk about you. Who will you be?"

Suki thinks for a second with her head tilted and then she says, "I'll be your friend."

"Why?"

"Because that's what I want."

I don't know what to say. I bury my face in her fur, pretending that I am bowing before the Buddha. *Buddham sharanam gacchami… I take refuge in the Buddha…* Well, why not? Suki and me, both.

When we take a break from trying to meditate and are walking outside, Suki says to me, "Next time I'll be a warrior. You can sit on my shoulder."

I think she means we should exchange places. I don't answer. But I don't think I want to be a Burmese cat. All that worrying about what I'm having for dinner and whether I'll like it or not. And all that having to be nice to what is, after all, an alien species.

Of course, Suki knows what I'm thinking, but all she says is, "Ha!" and then once again, "Ha!"

When it's time to go back into the dome, she says, "Come on, let's go and zap the rats. This time for real. You can pretend you're meditating in your room."

"Suki, no! We're not allowed to zap the rats."

"Well, you can go back into that dome. I might go and talk to the rats."

"Talk to them?"

"Yes, why not? They're about all there is. The other meditators aren't allowed to talk. The Teacher is a voice on a videotape. And The Babbler and Kingsie and Magsie et al, well..."

She doesn't complete her sentence and I don't insist. I don't think it will be flattering.

Inside the dome I find myself wondering if Suki really loves me. She hasn't met Toadie yet. Perhaps she would find Toadie even more repugnant than The Babbler.

And then before I can hide Toadie Suki returns. She turns Toadie over with a paw. The poor thing shrinks into itself. It tries to cover its eyes with its paws. Thinks perhaps that if it can't see, it can't be seen. Pathetic!

"Leave Toadie alone," I say sharply.

I can hear The Babbler murmur, "Toadie's very sensitive. Have to be gentle." Princie starts barking. Clearly Toadie has some friends. I feel humiliated.

Suki doesn't say anything. She pats my face with her paw and nuzzles my chin. Then she settles down beside me in the perfect posture for a meditating cat: her front legs straight, her tail wrapped neatly around her and her head erect – like the sphinx. I follow her example, I straighten my back and try to balance my head properly on my shoulders.

15

Clever Monkey

On the tenth day, as Suki and I walk to the meditation dome, we see a marmalade cat lying on his back on the lawn with one leg pointed skyward. He's washing himself. There are no rats about. Suki and I glance at each other and carry on. Once we're settled inside the dome, Suki says to me, "I never met any of your menagerie before. I mean when I was alive and we lived at home. Did you just acquire them?"

"No, no, they've always been there," I tell her. "It's just that they hide. The meditation brings them out. When I'm trying to meditate they start buzzing around, or at least I become aware of their activity."

"Is that it then? Have I met them all?"

I think she's trying to brace herself against further encounters.

"Well, there's Clever Monkey," I say hesitantly. "But you won't meet her. She likes to stay in the background."

"What does she do?"

"I tidy up," Clever Monkey tells Suki.

"What do you tidy up?" Suki asks nicely.

"Oh, everything," Clever Monkey replies impatiently. "The Babbler's babblings. Call it censorship if you like. The Babbler says what children say and what grown ups learn to hide. And sometimes I do a bit of mending. Then there are Magsie's straws. Some don't evaporate, they just lie there."

"What do you do?" Suki asks.

"Well, I transmute them if I can, or sometimes I work on them and plait them into patterns."

"Oh, come on, CM," I butt in. "Kingsie does that."

"Kingsie goes for the obvious. I have to work like a scavenger at times," Monkey replies.

"So you're a Censor, an Alchemist, and a Scavenger. Anything else?" inquires Suki.

"Well, I try to do searches sometimes." She hesitates.

We wait for her to go on.

"Even when I tell Magsie what to bring, she sometimes brings something quite different. The trouble is I can't properly control any of them."

Then she blurts it out. "You see, I'm educated." And before Suki can question her further, she disappears into the shadows. Probably gone off to do some mending or transmute straws or root about in rubbish. There's something about Clever Monkey I don't feel entirely comfortable with. Unlike the others, she's — she's — she's so judgmental!

Suki senses that my mood has changed. She nuzzles my arm and does a little purr, but when that doesn't work, she says quietly, "Don't feel so bad about your menagerie. I expect everyone has a kingfisher, a magpie, a toad and all the rest lurking in the shrubbery."

"So when birds babble, do you think they're carrying on exactly like The Babbler?"

"Why not?" says Suki. "Didn't you hear the blackbird this morning drooling about the worm he'd caught? And then going on about all the worms he's caught in his life, and how he's probably the King of Blackbirds."

I consider this. So my inner life, and presumably everybody else's, is no better than the inner life of chickens in a chicken yard — a whack here, a peck there as the impulse arises. Only our inner life is robed in language. "Oh Sooks, we human beings are no better than you!"

I didn't mean to say it as baldly as that. Where was Clever Monkey? But Sooks isn't offended. "No," she says, "you're probably not. And perhaps you're not even any worse."

"Suki," I begin. I want to apologize for making unhelpful comparisons. But she's no longer in the dome. Probably gone to talk with Ratsie – if she can find him. They're getting quite friendly.

In the silence suddenly I hear someone sobbing. It's Clever Monkey. I want to ignore her, but she says, "Why don't you like me?"

What am I supposed to say to a question like that? "Because you think you're so clever," I tell her. "Cleverer than anybody."

"Not really," Clever Monkey sobs. "Just wish I was."

"Well, there you are then," I retort. "You just want to beat everyone. And the rest of us have to work hard so that you can."

"No, I want to be liked by everyone. I say clever things so that people will like me."

"Wow," I say unkindly. "You chatter just as much as The Babbler."

"My teeth chatter," Clever Monkey wails. It's true, her teeth are chattering. "I'm very afraid and I want approval."

"Just approval?"

"No, I want to be loved."

"Why?" I'm relentless in my questioning.

"Because otherwise I'll die."

I suppose now I'll have to cuddle Clever Monkey. She's not very cuddly and she's so very needy. Oh well. And what about my meditation?!

And so when Suki returns and tells me she's arranged a story fest that night, I'm not pleased. "What about my meditation?" I wail.

"Everybody's babbling," Suki informs me. "It's the tenth day. Listen."

It's true. There's a babble of voices coming from the bushes, the rooms, the dining hall.

"Yes, but we've been babbling all this time," I say plaintively.

"We all have something to say," Suki replies firmly. "You'll have to listen."

"You mean you're all going to talk to an audience of one?"

"Well, I've invited Ratsie."

I sit in the dome with my head in my hands. I think I'd rather meditate than listen to them!

Later, when I've gone to bed, I can still hear voices. The babble of their voices is like crocuses opening in the spring, but not as charming. I want to get some sleep. I know that as soon as all the other meditators have settled down, Suki will wake me up and say it's time for the Story Fest.

I do fall asleep, and she does wake me up. Kingsie and Magsie are perched on the end of the bed. Squirrel sits beside them. Princie is on the floor wagging his tail lavishly. Toadie is hiding under a corner of the coverlet, and I can just see Clever Monkey out of the corner of my eye. Suki is sitting beside me. She tells me to sit up.

"We have guests," she says. I prop the pillow behind me and do as she says. The door to my room is wide open. There's moonlight streaming in and in the moonlight I can see a V-shaped formation of rats. Ratsie's at their head. Each of them carries a white flag.

"It's all right," he calls. "We have been invited, but we're not coming in. We will stay out here in the fresh air and listen quietly."

16

The Story Fest

For a few moments no one says anything.

"Well," Ratsie says. "Who will begin? Empress Suki, will you take the lead?"

I look sideways at Suki. "Empress?"

"It's all right," she whispers back. "He's a bit confused about titles. He's just trying to be polite."

To Ratsie she's magnanimous. I wonder if she's taking the 'Empress' bit seriously. "No, no," she says, "this entire narrative is about me and those associated with me, what I think of them, what they mean to me. It's time we heard what you have to say. What is your story?"

Ratsie jumps at the chance. "Oh well, if you say so, Empress, and if you agree, Madame," this with a little bow to me.

"Please," I murmur. What else can I say?

"This is no fairy tale," Ratsie begins. "I wish to recount our history. And then if you will, I would like you to be our emissary to the outside world as we know that tomorrow you are going to leave."

"I don't know if I can be your emissary," I begin.

But Ratsie interrupts, "Just hear us out. And then do your best to broadcast our message. Please? Please!"

All the other rats take up his cry. "Please. Please." They're making quite a racket. Nobody's going to think that's the wind in the trees.

"Shush," I say hurriedly. "Shush. Yes. Okay. I'll see what I can do. What is your history?"

"Know then that there was a time when we and the humans were neck and neck in the race for dominance. The only advantage that the humans had was that they were much larger. Our scientists decided that we must breed for size. Experiments were conducted in a secret location. But wars occurred. We fought among ourselves. We were persecuted by the humans, and our aspirations and the experiment itself were almost forgotten. But we have heard rumours of extraordinarily large specimens of our kind on a remote island in the Indonesian archipelago. This coupled with the fact that the humans themselves are bent on destruction has given us new hope. We —"

"Wait a minute." Clever Monkey cries. "Why not elephants?"

"What?"

"Elephants," Princie repeats from the floor helpfully.

"What about them?" Ratsie says.

"Why didn't they become dominant?" Clever Monkey asks.

"Oh, because they didn't want to be, I guess. Not aggressive enough. Anyway, here's the message: would humans like to enter into a power-sharing deal with us? We would try to prevent them from destroying themselves and the two species could rule together. What do you say?"

"Oh, I don't think I'm empowered to speak on behalf of the whole human race," I tell him, "but somehow I don't think they'll accept your offer."

Ratsie is incredulous. "Are you saying that they would rather destroy themselves than join with us? Oh well, we can wait. Rats will rule."

"What about kingfishers?" Kingsie says suddenly.

"And magpies and birds in general?"

"And the other primates?"

"And cats." Suki adds. "Aren't you forgetting something?"

"Forgetting what Empress Madame?"

"I could zap the lot of you. And anyway, I thought you wanted to substitute rats for cats?"

"Empress, Madam, Lady, you are forgetting we lead a charméd life here. It is forbidden to zap us. Besides, this is a peaceful occasion. It is just that our understanding of our full potential has now been heightened. We are here to tell stories, recount histories and hope for a better future."

"I haven't got any stories, but I've got another nugget," the chipmunk says suddenly.

"Go on then," Kingsie encourages her.

The chipmunk sits back on her haunches, clasps her front paws together, shuts her eyes, and says solemnly: "*The ego is lonely. What is not the ego is everything and it is not lonely.*"

This makes Toadie shriek and dive under the bedclothes. I don't want Toadie under the bedclothes, but I don't want to make a fuss. Princie is on his feet and growling at the chipmunk, "Now look what you've done. You've hurt Toadie's feelings."

The chipmunk sticks out her tongue at him and when he makes a swipe at her, she climbs up the curtains.

"Enough, you two!" I shout at them. There's a tap on the wall. The walls are thin. Oh no, have we woken up the other meditators?

Everyone is quiet and Kingsie decides to take centrestage. "Look at what I've got." She throws an intricately worked egg on the coverlet. It's made of gold. She taps the golden egg, and it opens into two halves. A tiny mechanical bird perches on the eggshell. "Shall I sing of the world?" it asks, "or of the universe?"

"Of the world," Magsie says hastily.

The little bird puts its head on one side and pipes:

Poor old world —
like a bruised melon
it wobbles and whirls
   and wobbles and whirls
as though it was
      still very young.

Then, without waiting for applause, it dives into its shell and the two halves close over. Kingsie retrieves the egg and puts it into a pouch around her neck. She looks pleased with herself.

"Clever little thing," she murmurs happily.

Suki is nearly asleep beside me. I tug at her ear to wake her up.

It's time to wind up. "Well, thank you everybody," I start saying, when Clever Monkey interrupts.

"There are several of us here who haven't had our turn," she points out. "What about you, Princie?"

"No, no, I'm just a retriever. I just fetch what I'm told to fetch," Princie says from the floor.

"Yeah, and I just fetch anything at all," Magsie adds. "I haven't got a brain in my head." She doesn't seem bothered by it.

Princie isn't done yet. "Now that you've asked me to tell my tale, there are one or two things I could tell you. I'm not just an errand boy or a postal carrier. Sometimes I'm given such vague instructions that I'm forced to think for myself. I have to find out stuff. I — I have to sniff out somehow exactly what's wanted."

"And how do you do that?" Clever Monkey asks sharply.

"Well, I just sniff it out. I have a strong sense of smell. I remember once — it was one of my greatest triumphs —" Princie stops short suddenly and looks uncomfortable.

Clever Monkey begins to giggle nastily.

But for once I know what to do. I pat Princie. "It's all right, old boy. Once you dug up a chunk of the past and it was redolent. What enticed and frightened you was the smell of death."

"And tulips," Princie mutters pathetically.

"And tulips," I agree. "What goes on in the mind may be quite as difficult as what goes on in the world, but it's not quite the same. Time can be coaxed to go forward and backward."

"And sideways and all over the place!" Clever Monkey screeches. "And that's my problem! Have you any idea how much trouble the rest of you make for me? I am orderly, I am educated, I am organized, I think, I slot, I control, I connect, I even make patterns and write complex texts, but I function in CHAOS! Anything goes anywhere, falls anywhere, is junked for no reason, is kept for no reason, is filed and misfiled and triple filed for no reason at all and then it isn't labelled or the label falls off. I am your nanny, your office manager, your storekeeper, your kindergarten teacher, your cleaning lady, your boss, your typist and, what is worst of all, because you make it almost impossible, I am responsible for keeping you sane. And do you co-operate? You do not. There's kingfisher, preening on a branch all day long. All she cares about is anything that glitters like the scales on a fish."

"Please, Clever Monkey," the kingfisher tries to say, "that's not true," but the flood of Monkey's words sweeps her aside.

"And as for the magpie, if she brings one more straw that isn't actually necessary, I'll wring her neck!" Monkey carries on.

"Well then," retorts Magsie. "You can wring my neck and you can all drift about in time and space. The straws make it possible to weave the future out of the past so that at least there's a semblance of continuity. Can't you see that?"

"Ha!" cries Clever Monkey. "A randomly accessed past cobbled together with a fictitious future! And you expect me to continue sane?!"

"Well, no," says the chipmunk. "We don't expect it."

Monkeyji fills her lungs and is getting ready to blast off again, when I clap my hand over her mouth. "If you don't lower your voice, you'll wake everyone. But before that happens, I'll throttle you," I tell her. "Give somebody else a chance to speak."

Clever Monkey subsides temporarily, and I call on

Toadie to say something. At least it will get the creature out of my bed.

"I'm scared," Toadie whimpers from under the bedclothes.

"Well, if you weren't scared, what would you say?"

"I would say, 'I am not scared.'"

"Is that all you can say? 'I am scared' and 'I am not scared?'"

"Yes." Toadie dives deeper into the bedclothes, then peeps out from under the covers. "I can also say 'I like' and 'I don't like,'" Toadie adds slyly, "but nobody pays any attention to me anyway."

"Oh rubbish!" Suki snorts. "You're their master. They all serve you. You're such a hypocrite!" She flicks Toadie out of the bedclothes. Toadie sprawls on the bedspread, completely exposed for a moment or two, then hides under a fold.

The others don't like what has happened. What Suki has said is true, but they're all very protective of Toadie. On the other hand they don't want to take on Suki. Ratsie and his cohorts watch from a distance. The sheer lack of noise is both strange and pleasing. It only lasts a moment.

"If no one else has anything to say, I have something to say," Clever Monkey announces in a loud voice. She actually stands where everyone can see her. I look at her critically. Not very pretty, but then primates never are. I suppress the thought and pay attention.

"Understand this," she begins. "If seven monkeys tried for 700 million years, they still would not produce the works of Shakespeare. They might produce a few correct sentences that said something sensible. And that would be about it. I am in charge of the 700 monkey or the 700 million monkeys typing. I have to sort out what they produce. It's too much. I am overtired and overworked."

"I thought The Babbler?"

"Yes, The Babbler is attached to 700 machines with monkeys typing. Have you any idea how much nonsense you produce? You will have to learn to discipline yourselves. I can't cope."

She really does look tired. "Well, that's why I was trying to learn to meditate," I say defensively, "but the babbling –"

All of us realize that The Babbler is missing. Instinctively we look at Clever Monkey.

"What did you do with The Babbler?" Suki asks sternly.

"Yes, what did you do?" Toadie asks in a frightened voice from under the covers. "Did you murder him?"

"No, I didn't murder him," Clever Monkey says defiantly. "I just knocked him out so that I could have some peace and quiet."

"And the 700 monkeys?" Suki asks.

"They've gone to sleep with their heads on their desks. They were tired."

"Get her, Princie!" Toadie shrieks from under the bedclothes. "I need The Babbler. He makes me feel better."

Princie lunges at Clever Monkey. She leaps for the curtain rail. Kingsie and Magsie fly about. Toadie emerges and balances somehow on Princie's back. Princie runs round and round in circles. Toadie falls off. Suddenly in an act of sheer courage or sheer desperation Clever Monkey jumps on Princie's back and growls at him, "Down, Princie!" Princie subsides. From under the bed Toadie giggles nervously. Eventually they settle down. Suki and I can go to sleep.

"Don't forget my message!" Ratsie calls over his shoulder as he and his troops march away, their white flags fluttering in the moonlight. For a moment I think that they are not unlovely; then my vision readjusts itself.

"Tomorrow we go home," I say to Suki.

"Whew," murmurs Suki.

17

The Return

The next morning the course is officially over. We've learnt what we've learnt. We can go home. "I've got to change trains three or four times," I say to Suki. "Why don't you do a Cheshire – no, I mean, slip through space time at the speed of thought? I'll meet you at home?"

"That's all right," Suki says. "I'll keep you company." She pauses. "What about the mountains?"

"What mountains?"

"You promised me an adventure," Suki replies. "The mind has mountains you said. I thought we were going on a Himalayan trek – something glorious or at least glamorous."

"Well, there are different sorts of minds. I'm not

Hopkins. But I have panic attacks sometimes. There's an abyss."

"An abyss is not a mountain," Suki says. She looks disappointed.

"Where there's an abyss, there's always a mountain," I tell her firmly. "Depends on where you're standing. Look, I've got to be helpful and do a few chores, and then we can go."

And soon enough we're ready. There's an eight-seater taxi for ten people. A mix up. A taxi didn't come. We scrabble for a place. We're ashamed and humiliated at having to scrabble after ten days of meditation. "The two who didn't get on aren't humiliated," Suki points out. No, they're enraged.

Suki and I have a fellow meditator accompanying us part of the way. He's pleasant and civil, but eventually he begins to talk about what is bothering him. He says he can't understand why he hasn't been granted instant Enlightenment when he wants liberation so fervently, so desperately. Why can't he be a Bodhisattva now? Wow! I make a mental note that when someone else babbles, The Babbler, my Babbler, must be silent perforce. Perhaps listening is good practice for meditation? And perhaps children don't ever grow up, they merely learn to shut up?

"Yes, but at least he knows what he wants," Suki says suddenly.

We wander through fields dotted with sheep, we

go through tunnels, we cross rivers, we get off at train stations and run across platforms to catch trains and at last we're in Devon on the home stretch. I like Devon. It probably has the most pleasing landscape of all the counties, though Dorset isn't bad. Gill meets us at the station and asks how the course went. "I worked hard," I tell her. Well, in a way I did.

Once we're home, Suki and I go straight into the study. She jumps up and examines my desk. "New printer," she comments.

She's waiting for me to open the top right-hand drawer. It's a mess. There's a jumble of things inside it: an old mobile phone, various cards, scraps of paper, a small book, a compass, a couple of pencils, some tape. Suki waits for me to clear it all out. "Where's my orange shawl?" she demands.

"Suki, when you were cremated, I asked that you be wrapped in it."

"So that I would be comfortable?"

I don't know what to say. "I'll get you another one," I mutter.

Once she's settled, she turns to me. "Well," she says, "are you going to give up meditating?"

"Well, no. I quite like it," I reply defensively.

For a while she doesn't say anything. Then she says, "You're not very good at it. As soon as you sit down, Magsie zips about, The Babbler starts up, and every now and then Toadie screeches."

"That's true," I admit. "But there's Kingsie and the chipmunk. They find some good stories, even poems sometimes. And somewhere in the wings there's Clever Monkey sorting furiously."

"You're supposed to be watching sensations rise and fall, rise and fall," Suki points out, "not stories."

"Why can't I watch stories rise and fall, rise and fall?" I sound petulant.

"It's mostly The Babbler you're listening to. And you hate The Babbler. You get exasperated with him. You want him to shut up. But The Babbler's mechanical. Nothing stops him."

"Suki, perhaps the Mad Mechs aren't creatures, perhaps they're robots, and my mind is a mindless machine?"

"No, no," Suki says kindly. "Sometimes what you say is quite interesting. And besides, there's always a reality check. I stop you, you know, when you go too far."

"But Suki," I blurt out, "you're only a memory."

Astonishingly, she isn't offended. "It all helps," she says peaceably.

I'm feeling bad about the way the menagerie behaved last night. "About last night," I begin, "they weren't –"

"Well-behaved," Suki finishes for me. "Never mind. Farce is better than nightmare. You're all right."

"Sometimes I think that without The Babbler there would be no stories."

"You're too attached to your stories."

"Yes. And to you. What's wrong with attachment, anyway?"

"There's nothing wrong with it," Suki says impatiently. "It's just that it's not helpful."

"You know, Suki," I tell her thoughtfully. "It's not just that I'm attached to you. It's worse than that – I'm attached to attachment."

"Well, in that case, why don't you give it up? Trying to be detached and equanimous and aware all at the same time?"

"Well, because I want that as well." I feel very stupid. "Suki, I think I want to be half liberated."

"If that's what you want, that's what you'll get — the wanting, the getting and the losing — over and over again."

Did she really say that? She's not always that blunt. I think she's asleep.

After a while she says, "Let go."

"Let you go?"

"Being attached."

I don't reply to that.

Then I say, "But I want my companionship with you. In it there's well-being and I feel engaged." I'm sounding querulous.

"Am I really here?" she asks gently.

"But Suki! Well, next time around?"

"Yes."

"Well, then au revoir?"

"Yes. Perhaps." She sounds sad for me.

"Yes."

"It would be better —"

"But then where would you be?"

"I would be where I always was," she says quietly.

"All right I will try to meditate. Morning and evening I will do my two hours. But Pook?"

"Yes?"

"Sometimes when I'm sitting will you come and sit with me?"

Suki laughs. "Of course, I will. I'll sit with you now."
She hops out of the drawer and sits on the floor with her
tail curled neatly around her. I sit down next to her.

After a while she opens her eyes. She looks at me and
suddenly she says, "Howdy pardner?"

I can't help laughing. Roy Rogers and the golden
palomino? Butch Cassidy and the Sundance Kid? Who
will we be next time around?

Somewhere at the back of my mind the kingfisher
starts up: '*The blossoms of the apricot—*'

"That's borrowed," I whisper.

"Never mind. It's soothing," she whispers back, and
starts again:

> '*The blossoms of the apricot*
> > *blow from the east to the west,*
> '*And I have tried to keep them from falling.*'
> > > Ezra Pound, Canto 13